"What's going on?" Ed asked.

"How should I know?" Celia replied. "The animals have gone crazy!"

"That's just it," Ed said slowly. "They haven't gone crazy. It's like they planned this—all together." He stared out of the cage at the closest tiger. Several deer stood near it, apparently unbothered. "Those deer should be terrified of the tiger—but they're not," he said slowly. "It's like they're working together."

"That's crazy!" Celia protested. "They're just animals!"

"I know." Ed was getting more and more scared by the moment. This shouldn't be happening. It couldn't possibly be happening. Except that it was.

The animals had taken over.

The Outer Limits™

A whole new dimension in
adventure . . .

THE OUTER LIMITS™

THE PAYBACK

JOHN PEEL

Tor Kids!

A TOM DOHERTY ASSOCIATES BOOK
NEW YORK

HAYNER PUBLIC LIBRARY DISTRICT
ALTON, ILLINOIS

This is a work of fiction. All the characters and events portrayed in this book are either products of the author's imagination or are used fictitiously.

THE OUTER LIMITS #11: THE PAYBACK

A Tor Book
Published by Tom Doherty Associates, Inc.
175 Fifth Avenue
New York, NY 10010

Tor® is a registered trademark of Tom Doherty Associates, Inc.

ISBN: 0-812-57568-7

First edition: May 1999

Printed in the United States of America

0   9   8   7   6   5   4   3   2   1

ADE - 3244

This is for Nicole Elizabeth Conniff.

Prologue

THE ANIMAL SHALL not be measured by man. In a world older and more complete than ours they move finished and complete, gifted with extensions of the senses we have lost or never attained, living by voices we shall never hear. They are not brethren, they are not underlings; they are other nations, caught with themselves in the net of life and time, fellow prisoners of the splendor and travail of the earth."

—Henry Beston, "The Outermost House" (1928)

People have very different views of animals—some see them as pets, others as wild and proud, and most of us see at least some of them as food. But how do animals see us? And . . . will their opinion of us ever change?

One thing is for sure—if they can be considered "other nations," then nations of the Earth often declare war on one another. If there were such a war, who would win?

CHAPTER 1

PENELOPE HATED MEN—all men. Naturally, she didn't let the men know this. She might be filled with hatred of them, but she didn't underestimate them. If they knew she hated them—and, especially, if they knew just how much she hated them—they would be furious. And then they would punish her even more than they already had. No, Penelope knew that she had to keep her hatred concealed, until the time came when she could do something constructive. Or, better yet, destructive . . .

She liked to watch men work. She would sit, pretending to do what they wanted, but she was really watching them. Her eyes followed their every movement, missing nothing. And she remembered everything that she saw.

She knew that, one day, her knowledge would be useful. Perhaps that day would be today.

Of course, she was limited in what she could do, at least for the moment. Since she was naked in a cage, they thought she was harmless. Well, that and because she was a monkey, of course. The men knew she had sharp teeth and a wiry strength, so they were very careful of her because of that. What they didn't know yet was that she had a mind, too. The humans believed that only they had intelligence, and perhaps they had once been correct in that belief.

But they weren't any longer.

Pretending to be studying the pictures they were showing her, Penelope was actually listening to the men talk. She had only been able to understand English (which is what they called their language, she'd discovered) for about two days. Three days ago, it had been nothing but noise, but then something had happened, and somehow Penelope had started to realize that the noises made sense, of sorts. They were made up of words, and words had meaning. For the past two days, she'd been listening as best she could, and making sense of what she was able. Now, though she understood the sounds, she didn't always know what the words meant. It was hard to get much of a perspective on things when your whole life was spent either in a cage or a laboratory.

"The subject appears to be making a decision," one of the men said. Penelope pretended not to be looking at him, but she knew this was the younger man. Like all men, he was virtually bald, with only tufts of hair on the top of his head. Quite grotesque, really. No wonder humans wore the coverings they called *clothing*—all of their hair seemed to have fallen out. But clothing had other uses, she knew. The men carried things in small cloth pouches known as *pockets.* She almost wished she had pockets, so that she could hide and carry things too. *The subject* was how he named her; he never referred to her as *Penelope,* though the older man sometimes did.

"She'll work it out," the older man predicted. He was only slightly different from the younger man. He had less hair on the top of his head, but he had some around his mouth. And it was all white, which was a very silly color. "She's very smart."

Penelope knew that he meant that she was smart *for an animal.* Not smart like a human, of course. But the older man was wrong—she was a whole lot smarter than even he guessed. Penelope knew that she was supposed to hit the yellow button and then the red button in her cage twice each to get a treat. She could have done it instantly, but if she had, the men would have been suspicious. They wanted her to be bright, but not *that* bright. So Penelope was pretending to think, while she was slyly watching them.

They both had *tape recorders* with them. These were small machines that, if you spoke into them, remembered your words, and spoke them back later—and in exactly the voice you had used! They were some sort of magic, of course, but Penelope was determined to understand man's magic and use it. If she spoke into a tape recorder in Ape, would it be able to talk back in the same language? Or could it only speak human?

She'd dragged this out as long as she dared. While she didn't want to look too bright, neither did she want to seem too stupid. If the men thought she wasn't very clever, they would switch her to some other line of experiments. Maybe the one they put Solomon on when he'd bitten one of them. Penelope had seen him two days ago, his skull shaved, a metal wire in his head, and all his personality gone.

She would never allow the humans to do that to her. She promptly pressed the right buttons twice each. A drawer opened in the side of her cage with a treat in it. She didn't have to pretend to enjoy gobbling it up. The men never fed her quite enough, and hunger was always a dull edge in her mind and stomach.

"Ninety-four seconds," the younger man said with some satisfaction. "That's a record. I really believe the drug is working." Penelope wasn't sure what a *record* was, but she knew by now what a *drug* was. They were kept in bottles on the shelves of the laboratory, and some were kept in cooling boxes. The men injected the drugs into the various animals they kept, and then waited to see what effects the drug would have.

Sometimes the drugs caused terrible pains. Penelope had heard many animals screaming in agony. Not just monkeys, but rats, and squirrels, and dogs, and rabbits. Some of the creatures were just names to her that the men had used, but she had seen some of the animals. And she knew that they had to hate the men as much as she did. Of course, she couldn't be certain, because she couldn't talk to the animals. Only the other monkeys spoke Ape, and most of them didn't speak it very well.

Penelope knew why that was. She had been given one of the experimental drugs four days ago. It had hurt, and her arm had felt as if it were burning up. She'd screamed almost the whole night. But then, the changes had begun. That was when she started to understand the men when they spoke. And when she could concentrate her mind and understand things.

The drug had changed her. It had made her smarter—a lot smarter. Smart enough to know that if she let the men know how clever she was, they would be furious. They would be afraid. And they might even destroy her. She was smart enough now to keep her intelligence mostly hidden. She realized that the humans didn't know that the drug had made her cleverer. Its purpose wasn't clear to her—something about a *counteragent* to *HIV,* whatever that was. *HIV* seemed to be something that affected humans, and made them sick, or less clever, or something. And the drug she'd been given was to fight that.

Because Penelope was careful, though, the men didn't yet know that it had made her smarter. Much smarter. And she intended to keep it hidden from the men. She'd heard the cleaners at night making jokes about "dumb animals," and she knew that this was what she had to pretend to be. There was no such thing, humans believed, as a *smart* animal. And she didn't want them to find out how wrong they were, because she knew what that would mean.

Pain or death.

That was what men were best at—giving out pain and death. Penelope had no desire for either, so she was walking a careful line, avoiding looking either too bright or too stupid. Just middling, to keep the men happy. And to keep her alive and out of pain.

The younger man looked at his watch. This was another magical machine that seemed to tell him information without using words. Somehow, it managed to tell the men what *time* it was. Time was how the day changed to night and back again. Since any idiot could see what time it was, it showed how pathetic humans were that they needed a magic machine to tell them things.

"It's almost dinner time," the young man announced. "We'd better pack in for the day." He slipped his tape recorder into his pocket. Of course it was almost dinner time! How stupid the man was, if he needed a watch to tell him that! Her stomach told her without any help!

"Right," the older man agreed. "I'm pleased with the progress Penelope is making. So far, BZT seems to be totally effective. We may be able to move on to further subjects soon." He used a piece of metal that he called a *key* to lock up everything by Penelope's cage, and then placed the key in one of his pockets.

As the men turned away, Penelope's hand shot out. She slipped the key from the man's pocket, and into her cage, under her foot. The man, of course, didn't notice a thing. Their senses were so crude, really. Without their magic, men could never survive, let alone dominate animals the way they did. As soon as the men left the room, Penelope relaxed. That had been the most dangerous part of her plan. She knew that if the men had caught her stealing the key, they would have punished her severely.

Now came the hard part: waiting. She didn't dare do anything while the men were still around. If they caught her outside of her cage for any reason, she'd be in terrible trouble. The feeders would be coming around soon. Penelope slipped the key into her bedding, which they wouldn't touch, and forced herself to wait.

Eventually, the men brought the food around, and changed her water. She didn't have to pretend to be enjoying the food, and eating it passed some time. When she was done, she sat watching the big watch on the far wall. The security guard always came around when the pointed sticks on the watch were in the same position. After that, the lights would be lowered, and nobody would be in here until the following morning. She'd have about twelve hours to work in, which ought to be plenty.

"Whatcha doin'?" Samson called. He was a smallish chimp two cages over. He couldn't speak too well, but he was curious and eager. He must have seen her take the key.

"Waiting," she informed him. "When the man with the gun has gone, then I'll show you something interesting."

Samson bared his fangs in a grin. "Can I play?"

"Soon," she promised him.

The guard came, looked briefly around the room, and

then turned down the lights and left. Penelope forced herself to wait just a little longer, in case he'd forgotten something and came back. Finally, she decided that she was safe. She collected the key and used it to open her cage. Then she placed it beside the cage and stepped out.

"Hey," Samson said in delight. "Cool. Let me out, too, huh?"

"Not tonight," Penelope told him. He wasn't smart enough yet. She knew he'd trash the place, and the scientists would know that something had been happening behind their backs. "But soon." Samson didn't like being put off, and he grumbled, and settled down in a huff. Penelope ignored him and went about her mission.

She crossed the room quietly, ignoring the noises of the other animals who were just as curious as Samson, and were all probably asking to be let out in their own peculiar languages. She headed for where the drugs were stored. The BZT was inside the cold box, and that was locked, but not with any key. You had to hit numbers on a small pad to make it open. The scientists hid those numbers from the other men, but they didn't bother hiding them from Penelope. They thought she would never remember them, or know what to do with them. But the men were wrong.

She tapped in the numbers, and the cold box opened. Inside was a rack containing twenty glass tubes of BZT. She took one from the back, and looked at it. Perfect! Now she went to one of the storage drawers and took out a hypodermic needle. She knew only too well how these worked—from personal experience! Carefully, she filled the syringe from the BZT, and set it aside. The empty tube she now filled with water and replaced it in the cold box. Then she locked it. The men would never know it had been opened.

Taking the hypodermic, she hurried to Samson's cage. He looked at her with fear in his eyes. "Whatcha doin'?" he demanded.

"Helping you," she told him. "I have to give you an injection."

"Hate them."

"I know you do," Penelope said soothingly. "So do I. But I'm not a man. You can trust me. This will make you smarter. Smart enough to fight the men with me."

"Fight?" That interested Samson. He shambled forward, and allowed her to give him a dose of the BZT. "Now I am smart?"

"Not yet," she told him. "But soon. Only, you have to be sure that the men don't find out how smart you are. You have to hide it from them, the way I do."

Then she moved on. She couldn't speak to the cats, of course, so she simply had to inject them, avoiding their hissing mouths filled with teeth, and their long-reaching claws. The two rabbits didn't even have the energy to protest. The other animals yelped and complained, but she managed to get them all before the syringe was empty.

Then she carefully disposed of it in the men's garbage. It would be collected first thing in the morning and disposed of promptly. The scientists wouldn't know there was an extra syringe in there, and the men who collected the garbage didn't care. Penelope was safe.

Finally, reluctantly, she returned to her cage. It was the hardest thing in the world for her to lock the door again, sealing herself in. But the men mustn't know that there was a problem yet. Not until she had her army of helpers.

It took all of her willpower for her to force her fingers to open. The key dropped to the floor with a heart-wrenching *clink*. When the men came in the following morning, the older man would think he had dropped it when he was putting it in his pocket.

He would never suspect the truth.

Until it was too late . . .

CHAPTER 2

"GOOD GIRL!" Spice looked around happily at the words of praise, her tongue lolling, her ears flopping, her tail wagging. Devra Thomas couldn't help loving her dog; she was just so happy and enthusiastic. Who couldn't love a dog like that?

Spice's original owner, obviously. Devra had found Spice, thin, starving, and infested with ticks, beside the road a year and a half ago. Scared and sick, Spice had been too exhausted to run away. Devra's heart had gone out to the poor terrier, and she had carried the small, shivering animal home with her. Mom had balked a bit at first, but seeing the terrible state the dog was in, she couldn't say no to Devra's looking after her. She'd even gone to the local store to buy food and dishes, while Devra gave the dog water and comfort.

That was the problem living in a tourist area like the Florida Keys. Too often tourists abandoned unwanted pets when they went home, assuming that somebody would adopt them—or not caring that they'd simply die. How could people be so cruel? Well, Devra knew it was so, even if she could never understand how anyone could bring themselves to be so cruel to a helpless animal.

And, after eighteen months, Spice was a very different dog. She'd filled out, and regained her trust—love, in fact—for Devra, and for Devra's mother. Spice seemed to know that the two of them had saved her life, and she was utterly devoted to them. She was also often underfoot, but even Mrs. Thomas could live with that. And Spice had her uses. Devra's mother owned and operated a small restaurant, and Spice helped to keep down the vermin. It was her job, and she took it very seriously. Anything larger than a locust would be hunted down. Those fast enough learned never to come back. The slower ones, like the lizard Spice had caught and shaken to death, didn't survive to learn.

Devra disposed of the corpse, since she had no desire to see scattered portions of it around the house for the next few days, and gave Spice a treat. Spice wolfed it happily down, and then returned to sniffing all about the place in case there were other invaders.

The bell rang, and Devra ran to answer it. She grinned as she saw it was Heather and Ed, two of her closest friends from school. There were only two more days of vacation left, and then it was back to the grind. Heather insisted that they make the best possible use of those days. Heather was like that—full of life and energy. She had blonde hair as bright as the sun (Devra joked that's where she stored solar energy), in contrast to Devra's short, dark locks. Heather's brother, Ed, was more sandy, and more solid. He ambled where Heather ran; he grinned while Heather prattled on. He was a good friend, and a quiet, solid rock of a teen. The three of them had been together for years now, a team always.

"Come on, lazy bones!" Heather called. "It's time to be out doing things."

"Things?" Devra repeated. "What things?"

"Any things!" laughed Heather. "The weather's excellent, and the day's a-wasting. Move your feet, Dev, and let's go!"

Devra smiled at her friend's impatience. "Okay." She glanced around at Spice. "Stay here, girl," she ordered. "Be good. No eating visitors, okay?" Spice ignored her, still intent on her hunting. Devra left the house, falling in with Heather and Ed. "So, what do we do?" she asked.

As they walked down the tiny street in Nolan called Main Street, Heather shrugged. "Dad's got business, so he couldn't drive us to the mall," she said. "Still, I'm all set for school anyhow, and there's not much else to do there."

"There's boys," Devra answered.

"There's a boy here," objected Ed.

"You don't count," Heather replied. "Not for what we want."

"Besides," Devra added, more kindly, "there are girls

there, too. And you're cute enough to get one if you want.''

"Can't," Ed replied. "Mom told me no more pets."

"Idiot!" Devra punched him gently on the arm. "So, if the mall's out, what are we going to do?" She waved to Old Man Cully in the bait shop.

"There's always the beach," Heather said, without too much enthusiasm.

"I didn't put on my suit," Devra objected. "Besides, even if it is the end of the season, it'll be too busy."

"And we do it all the time," Ed agreed. "Our last two days should be filled with something more memorable than catching a few rays."

"I'm open to suggestions," Heather replied.

"How about the animal farm?" Ed suggested. "I'll even treat."

"Wow! Such generosity!" mocked Devra. But she liked the idea. "We haven't been for a while, have we?"

"And we all know how much you enjoy animals," Heather added. She pretended to sigh. "Well, I suppose I *could* tolerate another visit."

"That's the spirit." Grinning, Ed led the way down the side road to the animal farm.

Devra was pleased with his offer. She knew he'd suggested it to make her happy, and it did. She loved watching the animals. The place was too small to be called a zoo, but it was a step up from a petting zoo, at least. Most of the animals there were pretty common, but there were a few interesting ones. Devra wished that Mom made enough money for them to be able to take really major vacations in Africa or some other country where the wildlife was interesting. But the restaurant was just popular enough to provide them with a living. And, of course, it meant that they could never leave town during the vacation seasons. Most of Devra's own vacations were short and local. Disney World was prominent among them, especially now that they had added Animal Kingdom to the attractions.

Ed paid for them to get in, past the African village–themed entrance, and into the farm itself. It covered about five hundred acres, but a lot of that was either the administration areas or undeveloped land. There were always rumors that the farm was going to grow, but if it did, it was growing very slowly. Most of the cages and enclosures had been here since Devra had first come as a child.

The deer milled around in their large enclosure. You could go in and feed them (for a fee, of course!), but she found deer kind of dull. She preferred more exotic species. The gibbons were more interesting, even if they did look bored sitting in the cage and grooming one another. One of the males tended to break the monotony by watering any unwary spectators who ventured too close, however, so anyone who went more than once stayed well back. Devra had been caught once, when she was six, and was careful enough now!

Her favorite area was the Night World enclosure. This was the only building in the park where real money seemed to have been spent. It was where all the nocturnal animals were kept, including a large bat cave, with bats allowed to fly free. That always fascinated her. And the fennec foxes in their fake burrows, with their large ears, and intelligent faces. And, of course, the red pandas.

The three of them lingered in here before heading out into the light again. Devra blinked at the sudden return to bright Florida sunshine, and she shielded her eyes, reaching in her bag for her sunglasses. As she did so, she saw movement in one of the trees fringing the area. It was brief, but she frowned.

"One of the monkeys must have gotten loose," she said, pointing at the tree. "There's one up there."

"I don't see anything," Heather complained, following her gaze. "Maybe it was a bird."

"With *fur*?" Devra asked. "Maybe we should tell someone." She looked around for one of the college kids who worked here during the summer. She hoped to be able to get a job here in a couple of years, too. But there was no sign of anyone to report her sighting to. And maybe Heather was right; maybe it had just been an optical illusion. This place was a bit cheap, but she'd never heard of any of the animals getting loose.

"How about one of *my* favorite animals next?" Ed suggested. "Hot dogs!"

"Sounds good to me," his sister agreed. "I'm starving. Come on!"

They headed for the food kiosk, which was close to the entrance. Devra was ready for a snack, too. The food here was pretty plastic—they often joked that they were served what the animals refused—but it was okay when you were hungry. Munching hot dogs with sauerkraut, and sipping sodas, the three of them sat at the rickety picnic tables provided.

"It almost makes you nostalgic for school cafeterias," Ed said, examining his hot dog. "I wonder what's in this thing? Kangaroo meat?"

"It wouldn't surprise me," his sister answered. "It keeps trying to jump back up my throat." She pretended to be gagging. Devra had to stifle a laugh. To avoid snorting cola through her nose, she looked away.

And saw the movement in the trees again.

"There *is* an escaped monkey!" she exclaimed, pointing. Heather and Ed looked where she gestured, and they both looked startled.

The creature was quite clear now, moving through the branches, as if heading with a purpose in mind. It looked quite small, but it must have escaped its cage.

"We'd better tell somebody," Ed decided. He glanced around, but there were no attendants in sight. "The kiosk," he decided. They ran together to the food kiosk.

"One of the monkeys has escaped," Devra said to the woman behind the counter. "It's in those trees."

"Drat," muttered the woman. "I'd better call for them to get it. It's not likely to hurt anyone, but we don't want a panic. Or some member of the public trying to grab it." She looked at the three of them significantly. "They can bite pretty nastily if they get scared, so stay away from it."

"As if we'd *want* to catch it," Heather muttered.

"That's odd," the woman said, tapping the phone several times. "The line seems to be dead. And it was fine just a couple of minutes ago."

Why did this place having phone trouble not sound surprising? Devra would have shrugged it off and gone on with her hot dog. Except . . .

The phone line ran beside the tree she'd seen the monkey in. Maybe it had somehow broken the wire by accident? It could have tried jumping onto it to escape, and it would have snapped under the animal's weight. In fact, she could see something by the tree, moving slowly in the breeze, that looked like a loose wire. She pointed it out to the woman.

"Great," she snapped. "I can't leave this place unattended, even to find somebody to tell."

"No problem," Ed volunteered. "We'll go find somebody. At least it's something to do. Come on, guys."

Devra looked at her hot dog and decided she could live without it. She tossed it into the nearest trash bin. To her surprise, there were no squirrels scavenging there. Normally the little pests were everywhere they might find food. And, come to think of it, no birds, either. Well, it couldn't be very important. She followed Ed and Heather as they walked down the pathway.

It led them by the trees, and Devra called a halt. She had been right—the wire *was* dangling. "The monkey must have broken it," she said. "Jumped on it and snapped it, probably."

Ed reached up and managed to snag the loose end. His face went tight. "No," he said slowly. "This has been *bitten* through. I can see tooth marks on the insulation."

Devra scowled. "That doesn't make any sense. Why would a monkey bite through a phone wire?"

"I don't know," he confessed. "Maybe it was trained to?"

"Who'd train a monkey to do a dumb trick like that?" Heather protested. "Not even those Free Animal fanatics that picket this place sometimes would do that."

"I'm getting a bad feeling about this," Ed said. "Look, you two head outside to the parking lot. There's a pay phone there. Try and call in from it." He pulled a handful of coins from his pocket and gave them to his sister. "Tell whoever you get what's happened. I'll try and find somebody in here, okay?"

"Anything to get rid of us," Heather said. Then she shrugged. "Sure, why not? It's your dime." She and Devra turned away.

Devra had a bad feeling about things as well, but it was just foolishness, she knew. They had to be over-reacting, but for some reason she felt safer heading toward the exit. Out of the main gate, Heather went over to the pay phone.

"The stupid monkey must have got this one as well," she complained. "No dial tone."

"There's one at the bait shop," Devra suggested. "I don't think the monkey could have traveled that far."

"I was only joking about the monkey," Heather replied. "It's probably just vandalism here. Somebody trying to get the coin box open."

"Maybe. Still . . ." Devra jerked in shock as she heard a scream from inside the game farm. And then another.

Then a whole host of screams.

"What's happening?" Heather said, sounding as scared as Devra felt. They both looked back at the main gates, expecting to see a bunch of howling people running out.

"Animal escape?" Devra guessed. "Maybe we should call the police?"

"We ought to know what we're calling about," Heather pointed out.

"You're welcome to go back and check to see if something dangerous is running around," Devra said. "It's not at the top of my list of things to do."

"Look!" Heather cried, pointing at the gate.

There *had* been an animal escape! Over the top of the wooden gate, Devra could see the head of one of the two baby elephants in the park. But it wasn't trying to get out of the park.

"It's closing the gates," Devra gasped. "But why?"

"It's locking people in," Heather whispered. "And Ed's still in there!"

Devra felt a stab of panic in her heart. There was still screaming going on inside the animal farm. What was happening inside those walls?

"We've got to get help for them," she decided. "Come on!" And she turned and started running as hard as she could for the bait store and the nearest telephone. She *had* to get help—she *had* to!

CHAPTER 3

WASHINGTON, D.C., IN September was a nice place to be. Not as many tourists, now that the kids were about to go back to school. And a lot of the foreign visitors were gone, too. Not that Colonel Alan Adair had anything personal against either foreigners or school kids. It's just that they tended to congest the transport systems and slow him down when he was in a hurry.

As he was now.

The summons to the Pentagon was sudden, but not exactly unexpected. Anybody contacting Colonel Adair did so because there was a problem. He had a very loosely defined job, which could best be described as "trouble consultant." Whether you wanted to start it or stop it, Alan Adair was the best man for the job. He enjoyed it, because it meant that every job was different, and every job was a challenge.

He had no idea why the Pentagon wanted to see him. It could be a covert op in Iraq, or a satellite retrieval in the Sahara. He'd find out, he'd make his plans, and then he'd do whatever was required of him. Or die trying.

The soldier on guard at the entrance examined Colonel Adair's card with extra care. *Must be on alert,* Adair decided. It bore all the signs. Terrorist attack? Threat of war? Or just some politician paying a surprise inspection so he'd look good on the evening news? Not likely the latter, or Adair would not have been summoned. Finally, the guard waved him through.

The colonel parked, removed his briefcase from the backseat, and then locked his car. He straightened his tie and placed his cap on his head. Then he marched smartly inside the main building. He was stopped and checked a further four times before he reached the office of General Halsey. To his surprise, he was announced immediately. That was almost unheard of—generals liked to impress you with how important their time was, and how gracious they were to share it with you. In other words, they made you wait until they were good and ready.

Which meant that something very urgent was up. His pulse raced, and a faint smile crossed his lips. This was likely to be a good assignment.

''Colonel,'' the general greeted him. There were two other people in the office. One was General Halsey's assistant, Lieutenant Barlow. The other was a woman whose dark, reserved clothing said *FBI*. That was interesting, because it meant that this wasn't purely a military mission. And since she was obviously FBI and not CIA, it meant it had to be somewhere in the U.S. and not overseas.

"General," he said, saluting. Then he nodded. "And lady." There were polite, worried nods, except from the woman, who seemed to be examining him with her dark eyes. *She's heard about me,* Adair thought, *and wonders if what she's heard is true.*

It was, of course. His military files wouldn't bear even a hint of flattery.

"This is probably a bad one," the general admitted. That he would say so in itself was scary. "Barlow, brief him."

The aide stood up, holding a remote control. Flicking buttons in quick succession, he shut off the lights, and brought up a projector screen. On the screen flashed an aerial photo of an island. It looked small, since there were several scattered buildings to give Adair some sense of the scale.

"Cobra Island, in the Florida Keys," Barlow said. "Drug and vaccine testing center. It went silent at four P.M. yesterday." Another shot, this time from the water, showing the island to be almost flat, save for the rise of roofs. "No word out, and we can't even raise a carrier. A boat was sent in to check. It didn't report in and hasn't returned."

Adair nodded. It had to be some sort of emergency

situation, of course, or he wouldn't be here. "Contamination hazard?" he guessed.

"Not likely," Barlow replied. "They work mostly with animal diseases, but also with HIV and other human strains. Biological materials may have escaped, but they're fairly isolated there. Animal testing, mostly. Forty-six people. Stringent security."

"Why? For animal diseases?" There had to be more.

Barlow shook his head. "They're one of the plague carriers."

Uh-oh. This was starting to make a great deal of sense now. Cobra Facility was one of the three places in the western hemisphere that kept samples of the Black Death. If that should get released, or fall into the wrong hands . . . it had once wiped out one third of the human race, and would probably do so again. "You said there's not much chance of hazard," he pointed out.

"The sample is in a secure area, passable only with electronic keys, coded to their wearers. It couldn't escape in any scenario we've run."

"Except deliberate release," Adair pointed out.

"Yes," the nameless woman said, finally breaking her silence. "We have no reason to believe that this was done, however."

Adair laughed. "And how much reason to believe it *hasn't* been done?"

She seemed pleased with his question. "Just as little."

Adair now understood what was going on. "When do I go in?" he asked. "And what's my team?"

"Just as soon as we can get you there," the general

snapped. "There's no time to waste. There's a chopper waiting to take you to your plane. Your equipment is already aboard. You parachute into the sea off the island, swim ashore, recon, and report in. If there's trouble, call for help. Fix it if you can, but don't be afraid to yell for help. Your team . . ." He nodded at the FBI agent. "Agent Parker. She's the biological expert. We daren't risk anyone else until we know what's going on."

Adair didn't like that piece of news. Not that he had anything in particular against Agent Parker, but he liked to work with people he'd gone through training with. When you had a new person along, you could never be sure how they'd react. On the other hand, he was too well trained to question orders. "Sir," he agreed, with a shade less than full enthusiasm. If the general noticed it, he didn't comment.

"This way," Barlow said, not even bothering to bring up the lights. He tossed the control aside, and led the way toward the helipad. Agent Parker fell in step beside Adair, her face as stony as ever.

"You have a first name?" he asked her.

"Yes," she replied.

After a moment, Adair grinned. He was starting to like this FBI agent.

The plane swung out over the Keys on its final approach. This was an Osprey, able to hover, thanks to its wings. The engines could swivel through ninety degrees, turning the plane into a helicopter. Adair and Parker would drop into the water from the Osprey at a safe distance from the island. Safe for the Osprey crew, of course. He and she were already in their wet suits, and Adair was running the final check on his equipment. He didn't need much, and this evidently bothered Agent Parker. As he strapped his knife to his forearm and slipped his silenced pistol into the protective sheath, he stared back at her. "Do you have a problem?" he asked, mildly.

"That's not much firepower if we're up against terrorists," she said.

"True. If there *are* terrorists down there, I don't aim to start a gunfight. You've been watching too many Arnold Schwarzenegger movies, Agent Parker."

She rolled her eyes. "Then what do you intend to do, Colonel Adair?"

"Two words," he answered, grinning. "Cunning and silence." She looked puzzled. "Look, the two of us couldn't fight off an army—and that's what you'd need to take that island." He'd studied the maps, of course, and the details on the security system. "And it's not your job to fight."

"I'm a trained agent," she objected.

"I'm sure you are," he agreed. "But, like I said, this isn't Rambo time. We'll sneak in, take a look, and use our trusty radio to alert the forces waiting for us. If there's any fighting, they're the ones who are paid to do it. We're paid for being brilliant, so let's stick with that, shall we?"

That silenced her. Moments later, the plane was in position. First out was the small inflatable boat with the virtually silent motor. Then Adair, and finally Agent Parker. She unbent enough to allow him to help her into the rocking boat. As he started the engine, the Osprey moved away.

He steered the boat toward the island. They were far enough out for the plane not to have been spotted—if anybody was watching. If this was a terrorist strike, of course, there was a good chance they'd have been in and gone. But there was a small chance that a bunch of fanatics might have crept in and decided to stay. In which case, they would be looking for trouble. Adair just hoped they wouldn't spot it.

They had no trouble going in. He scanned the island carefully as they drew closer, but there was no sign at all of any hostiles. Or of any other boats. They were about a quarter way around the island from the main dock, of course. But it was unlikely that terrorists would have struck through that. It was too well-guarded. As they beached the boat, Agent Parker jumped out to help him haul it into the nearest cover. Then he scrubbed the tracks from the sea. She handed him his sandals, and then they set off toward the alarm perimeter.

Agent Parker had a small monitor, which she held out before her as they approached the alarm site. "Dead," she said. "No power readings at all."

"Natural causes?" he asked. That got him a slight smile.

"Impossible to say. I'd have to check the main panel."

"I'll see if that can be arranged." He gestured with

the gun he'd been carrying since they hit the beach. "Ladies first."

"Gee, thanks." But she took the lead. She'd clearly memorized the maps as well as he had. She stayed clear of the paths, but headed for the main lab building.

Adair was worried. There was no noise except the sighing of the trees in the wind. No animals, no birds. There ought to have been *some* sounds, but there were none. This was trouble, he was certain, but what kind of trouble? The radio slung across his back seemed to be getting heavier, but there was no way he was leaving it behind. He might need to call in anything from reinforcements to a full military strike any time now. If it came to that, he'd have no hesitation to have the island flattened, even with the two of them still here. That was his job, and he'd never shrunk from his duty before this.

Agent Parker had another instrument out of her backpack now. This one was some sort of sniffer. Testing for biological agents, no doubt. After a moment, she looked up. There was a faint sheen of sweat on her stern face. She was human, then. He'd been wondering.

"No sign of any contamination in the air," she informed him.

"That's good, considering we didn't bring any bioharzard suits."

"If we were infected with the plague, Adair," she told him, "there would be plenty of time to treat us before we got sick. It isn't a very fast disease. Just a nasty one."

"You don't know how reassured I feel now." He waved her to silence, and took the lead. They were almost at the main lab now. He halted at the edge of the trees, and scanned the area in front of them carefully. There was no sign of anything wrong. But if a terrorist group had struck, they'd most likely hide any evidence, to sucker in people like him. He waited, refusing to be rushed, letting his eyes and ears do their work. Parker, thankfully, stood behind him, silent as usual. He was glad she wasn't a talker. And she wasn't impatient, because she said nothing, and barely moved, for fifteen minutes.

"I'm going in," he whispered. "Stay here and cover me. But I think there's nobody home."

She had her own gun out, and nodded. She understood the sense of his order, and saw no need to reply.

There was a trickle of sweat worming its way down his spine, but he ignored it. Adair wasn't fearless, but he refused to let his fears out. He took one last look around, broke cover and sprinted for the door. Any second, he expected to feel a bullet slam into some portion of his anatomy, imagining one cutting through an arm or a leg, or bringing him to the ground.

Nothing. He reached the door panting very slightly. That was all. There was some measure of relief in that, but this was just the first possible ambush site. He paused by the door, and then pushed it open, standing to one side in case of bullets. Again, nothing. He chanced a quick look inside, and then slipped in.

There was a small vestibule, with a receptionist desk and security equipment. Beyond that, a secure door— now gaping wide open. There was no sign of anybody, nor was there any sign of blood. That scared him, because no security guard should have given up without a fight. What had happened here?

Agent Parker joined him, her dark eyes scanning the place. "It's not right," she said. She had the indicator in her hand again. "No power at all. We'll have to pray there's lots of natural light."

"You pray," he said, raiding the security desk and coming up with a heavy duty flashlight. "I'll shine."

"And attract bullets."

He grinned. "That's my job." He stepped into the corridor, as she checked the air.

"Still no biohazard," she reported. He could hear the relief in her voice.

They moved slowly down the corridor. There was no point in checking every room, and no need. All of the doors were open, and there was no sign at all of life. Something about this wasn't right. . . .

It was Agent Parker who figured it out first. She tapped his shoulder and gestured at one of the side rooms. "Lab," she said. "But where are the animals?"

That was what had been bugging his subconscious, too. There were cages for test subjects, but all of them were empty. He played his flashlight over them.

"Green Earthers?" he suggested, but he knew that was stupid the second he said it. No eco-loving group could do anything like this. Greenpeace protested whaling, but they couldn't break into a top security installation and get rid of armed guards without a sign of struggle. Agent Parker knew it was a dumb thought, and just snorted.

The main lab was directly ahead. Adair stopped, his nostrils flaring. Finally, he could smell what he'd been expecting all along: blood. There would be bodies there, that was for certain. And perhaps their foes. He glanced at the agent, and saw she'd smelled the blood, too. Her face was as resolved as ever.

More carefully, Adair moved forward. He'd snapped off the flashlight, but there was plenty of illumination from skylights to see what was ahead. He waited by the open door, listening. There were no sounds, except for insects. After a moment, he could stand it no longer. He rolled across the doorway to the other side, his gun ready for action.

There was no need. He stood up, stunned, and simply stared at the fight in the lab.

All forty-six of the missing personnel were here. They were all dead. But they hadn't died easily. Some had scalpels through their eyes. Others had electrodes stabbed into their brains. Some had simply been hacked to death. All of them had died slowly, in agony.

Adair felt sick at the sight. Even stone-faced Parker looked pale. Who could have done this to the scientists? And, more importantly, were they still here?

CHAPTER 4

ED HAD TO really focus his mind to stop from panicking. The only comfort he had right now was that his sister and Devra were—hopefully!—safe out of this nightmare. The problem was that he was in the thick of it. All of the screaming around him didn't make trying to stay calm any easier.

The tigers had somehow managed to get free. There were three of them, normally in a strong cage or in their night quarters—in either case, behind several locks. How they had managed to get loose was impossible to say, but there was little doubt that all three of them were free in the park. Ed could hear them roaring, and all from different sides.

A mother with a stroller rushed past him, crying and trying to protect her baby. Though nothing was immediately chasing her, Ed understood her panic. There was obviously nothing he could do now to warn the staff that a monkey was loose—they had to be more concerned about the tigers!—so he turned, deciding to help the young mother.

It wasn't far back to the food kiosk, but it was no longer a cheerful place. There were yelling people milling about there, and Ed quickly saw why. Somehow, the exit gates were closed, and two elephants appeared to be standing guard there. They were only small, but very bulky. They were clearly not going to move, and raised their trunks, howling out their anger.

Standing guard? What was going on here?

"My baby!" the mother yelled. "I've got to get my baby to safety!"

Ed agreed, but what could they do? Even if everybody here rushed the elephants, they couldn't possibly push them aside. They were simply too massive and too determined. "Maybe there's another exit," he guessed. There was a board showing the park map nearby, and he hurried to it. Most of the people seemed to just be yelling, either in fear or anger. One man picked up a chair, and flung it at one of the elephants. The beast simply caught it in its trunk and smashed it against the ground.

"We've got to attack them!" the man yelled. "We've got to get out before we're clawed to death!"

Ed didn't give much for his chances. He concentrated on the map. It showed no other exits, but he saw that there was a road marked by the administration buildings. These lay to the north. The road probably left the park.

"We could try going this way," he suggested. "This place only has two elephants, and they're both here. Plus, that's where the guards will be, and I'm sure they have tranquilizer guns or rifles or something."

The mother shook her head. "That's past the tigers," she replied. "They'll kill us all!"

"If we stay here, they could just hunt us down," Ed pointed out.

"The guards will get them," the woman said, more in hope than belief. She pulled her baby out of the stroller, clutching it to her chest. "They've got to."

Ed wasn't as optimistic. He looked around. The angry man had managed to talk a couple of the other men into joining him in an attack on the elephants. Ed was certain this was foolish, but they were determined to try. Each had managed to tear strips of planking from the food kiosk. All three men rushed one elephant together.

The animal howled, and its trunk lashed out, catching the leading man. He fell to the ground, soundless, out cold from the blow. A second man managed to hit the trunk with his stick, and the animal bellowed in pain. Then it reared up and stomped down. The man didn't stand a chance. The elephant's weight came down on him, crushing him. Ed looked away, wincing at the sound of shattered bones.

Several of the women—and one or two of the men— screamed at this. The children were in hysterics. Ed felt sick and more scared than ever. The last of the three men dropped his stick and fled back to the crowd.

Ed looked around, avoiding the area by the elephants.

He could hear the tigers roaring still, and people yelling. But there was no sound of firing, as he'd have expected if the guards were trying to calm things down. They might not be the most alert people in the world, but they simply had to be aware of what was happening. There was no use in staying here, he decided. Risky as it was, he preferred to try and make a break for it. He eyed the heavy fence about the park with a sigh. Naturally, it was too tall to climb, and there was nothing to get hold of. The designers hadn't wanted any animals going over the walls. Now it effectively trapped the people, too.

Which left the road. He looked at the young mother, but she was crying hard and trying to comfort her baby. The infant was somehow not crying yet, but it wouldn't be long. "Are you coming?" he asked her. She shook her head. Ed shrugged, and started off alone.

The pathway led past the rest rooms, and then past one of the enclosures. He couldn't remember which one it was; deer, probably.

The gate was open, and nothing was left inside.

Were *all* of the animals loose? Had some maniac gone around, opening all of the cages? But how could anyone, and why? Surely not even the most freaked out animal rights fanatic would let out the tigers to kill people. And why were the elephants blocking the exit? He didn't have any answers to these questions, of course, so he concentrated on escape.

He could hear people yelling and screaming, but they all seemed to be closer to the center of the park. There was nobody on the path he'd chosen, and, so far, no animals, either. This whole business didn't make any sense at all. Why were all of the people apparently crowding together? Surely some of them must have realized that they stood a better chance of escaping on their own than in a bunch?

And then he saw one of the security guards. The man was on the ground, obviously dead. His head was half-gone. Ed fought back the vomit that wanted to escape. He saw that the man no longer had his gun or his keys. One of the tigers must have killed him. Ed looked around, shaking. Was the creature still here? Was he stalking Ed right now? Then he shook the terror off, because he could hear all three tigers roaring closer to the center of the park. They must be stalking the crowd there.

Besides, a tiger couldn't take the man's gun and keys. Somebody else must have realized that this was a likely way out, and stumbled across the body before Ed. And if there was someone with a gun up ahead, he could protect Ed as well.

Ed started off again. He wanted to run, but was scared that this would attract attention. Instead, he stuck to the side of the path, trying to lurk beside trees, shrubs, or anything available to hide. This place was insane, and he simply didn't know what to expect.

Certainly not what happened.

There was a chirping from a tree ahead, and Ed glanced up, seeing a monkey in its branches. It might have been the same one they'd seen earlier, but he didn't know. It was bouncing up and down on a branch and pointing at him.

Ed couldn't believe it. *The thing was singling him out!* He'd never heard of any animal acting like this. It was calling out to something that he was here! Ed didn't even want to think what it might be alerting.

He picked up a rock from the pathway border and flung it at the chittering monkey. "Get the hell out of here!" he yelled. The monkey just dodged, and the stone missed it. There was no point in trying to hide now, not with that traitor giving away his position. But to what? One of the tigers? Monkeys didn't cooperate with tigers, though! It was crazy to think it.

But this whole situation was crazy.

Ed gave up caution; he simply ran, fast and hard. He had to get out of this madhouse!

He didn't get far. Ahead of him, several of the deer blocked the path. Ed skidded to a halt, astonished, staring at them. They didn't seem skitterish and docile, as they normally did. More grim and purposeful. He glanced back the way he'd come and saw two more deer blocking his retreat.

Deer cooperating like this? He couldn't figure it out. And why would they be after him anyway? They were timid creatures. Resolved, he moved forward. "Out of my way!" he yelled, shooing at them with his hands. They stood firm, staring coldly back at him. Ed bent and picked up a handful of stones from the flower bed. He flung one at the closest deer. "Move!"

The deer yelped as it was hit, and then snorted. Putting

down its head, it charged Ed. Ed barely got out of the
way before it thundered past him, skidded to a halt and
whirled around. It butted him in the leg, and Ed yelled
with pain. His thigh went numb from the blow, and he
almost collapsed. He let the other stones fall, and that
seemed to calm the deer down a bit. It glared at him,
and butted him a second time, but almost gently, telling
him to move.

"Okay, I'm going," he said, breathing hard. The deer
followed him closely. The two others ahead of him
moved to either side. Ed realized with a sickness in his
stomach that he was being herded. He didn't understand
any of this. Why weren't the deer fleeing in panic from
the tigers? Why were they cooperating like this? Where
were they taking him?

There was a side path branching off that led toward
the center of the park. Towards, in fact, the tigers. The
deer behind him butted him to take the path.

"You've got to be joking!" Ed snapped, shaking.
"I'm not going near those tigers!"

The deer butted him again, less gently this time. Ed
tried to fight it off, but the other two joined in, flailing
him with their sharp hooves. He cried out as they cut
through his clothing and skin, leaving bloody trails.
Eventually, he had to give in and go the way they
wanted. He was hurting all over now and limping. He
couldn't believe that three deer, barely taller than his
waist, could get him so completely in their control.

They passed another dead guard. This one was missing

most of an arm, and seemed to have bled to death. Once again, his gun and keys were missing.

Then came the biggest shock of all. The pathway opened out into the main area of the game farm, where the largest, more dangerous animals were kept. These cages were occupied, though—but not by their former inhabitants. They were filled with crying, whimpering, or unconscious people. The animals were *outside* the cages. Including the three tigers and two brown bears.

The deer pushed Ed toward the closest cage. He looked around, and saw that other deer and a couple of the ostriches were herding other people toward cages, too. Chimps sat at the gates, the missing keys in their hands, letting in the prisoners and then relocking the cages.

"What the heck is this?" Ed muttered to himself. "A remake of *Planet of the Apes*?" The deer pushed at him, and he stumbled past one of the bears. It looked at him, a low rumble in its chest, but didn't attack. Ed was relieved to walk into the cage after that, past the watchful chimpanzee. Hearing the door locked behind him made him feel a little safer. At least there were bars between him and the bears and tigers.

People were huddled together, shaking and scared. Some had even wet themselves. Mothers clutched their young to themselves protectively. Babies howled in fear, and so did some of the adults. This was the tiger cage, and was about twenty feet across. Inside, there had to be more than fifty people.

He saw Celia Cameron, a girl he vaguely knew from

school. Her blouse was torn, and there were tooth marks on her exposed left arm. Her mascara had run from crying. Ed went over to her. "What's going on?" he asked.

"How should I know?" she replied. "The animals have gone crazy!"

"That's just it," Ed said slowly. "They *haven't* gone crazy. It's like they planned this—all together." He stared out of the cage at the closest tiger. Several deer stood near it, apparently unbothered. "Those deer should be terrified of the tiger—but they're not," he said slowly. "It's like they're working together."

"That's crazy!" Celia protested. "They're just animals!"

"I know." Ed was getting more and more scared by the moment. This shouldn't be happening. It couldn't possibly be happening. Except that it was.

The animals had taken over the game farm, and imprisoned the humans in their places—the ones who hadn't been killed. This was well thought-out, with the guards being disarmed and stopped. The monkeys had cut the telephone wires, and the deer and tigers had worked together to herd up the humans.

What was going on here?

And what did these creatures have planned for their captives?

CHAPTER 5

DEVRA AND HEATHER ran as fast as they could toward the bait store. There was no telling what was happening in the game farm, but they had to alert *somebody*. The police, for starters. Though Devra wasn't sure that the police would even believe them. Somehow, though, she'd make certain that somebody paid attention and did something.

Lots of vagueness to those thoughts, she knew. But it stopped her from worrying about Ed. Mostly.

The town seemed to be strangely quiet. Okay, it was the end of tourist season, but there should still be people all around. The locals with shopping to do, neighbors to chat to, lawns to water or cut. And the main street, when they hit it, seemed to be just as dead. There were no cars or passersby.

"I don't like this," Devra said, stopping and staring at the still street. "Where is everybody? They can't all be at the game farm."

"Maybe the police know there's something wrong and told everybody to stay indoors?" Heather suggested. But even she didn't sound convinced of that explanation.

"Then we'd have seen the cops heading for the game farm," Devra objected. The bait store was only a few hundred feet away, and the public phone on a pole outside it. "Come on, let's call for help." She half-walked, half-ran the rest of the way. She was feeling the strain of the panic and the dash for help. She snached up the receiver, and pressed it to her ear. Then she groaned. "It's dead, too."

"More cut wires?" asked Heather anxiously.

"I don't know." Devra hung it up. "It's just dead. Now what?"

"Let's ask in the store if we can use Old Man Cully's phone," Heather suggested. "Maybe that still works."

Devra didn't give much for the chances of that being the case, but she didn't have any better ideas. "Okay." Besides, at least Cully might be able to help them, come up with another idea or something. It was worth a try.

They entered the bait shop. Normally, Devra liked the place. Old Man Cully was a cheerful soul, even if he did tend to ramble on a bit with his fishing stories. His store was like its owner—lots of things, not necessarily in any logical spot. Fishing rods, gutting knives, nets, bait buckets . . . even bows and arrows and guns (all unloaded, though) for the would-be hunters of the area. And, always, Cully himself, ready with a tooth-impaired grin and a lot of improbable stories.

But now the store was deserted. Devra looked around uncertainly. Maybe he was in the bathroom? "Mr. Cully?" she called, loudly. There was no reply.

Heather moved determinedly behind the counter. "I'll explain later," she said, picking up the phone. "Damn!" She slammed it back down again. Devra didn't need to ask why; it had to be dead, too.

Were any of the phones in town working? Or were just the ones near the game farm cut? Maybe if she went home, their own phone would be working?

"Cell phones," Heather said suddenly, brightly. "At least one of the cars must have one."

"The cars will be locked," Devra objected.

Heather picked up a small hatchet. "I've got a key," she said with determination.

"Heather!" Devra said, shocked. "You'll get into trouble!"

"Trouble?" Heather laughed, almost hysterically. "Don't you think we're in trouble already? What do you need, some mad stalker to jump out of the gloom at you with a knife before you face reality? Something seriously wrong is happening! I'll chance getting yelled at for breaking somebody's window and using their phone!"

Devra wavered a moment, and then realized that her friend was right. This was no time to be polite and follow all of the rules. She snatched up the largest gutting knife she could see. Just holding it made her feel slightly safer. Of course, she couldn't fend off an elephant with it.

She eyed the shotguns on the wall. "Maybe we should take a gun?" she suggested.

"I'd be more likely to shoot myself than anything else," Heather confessed. "I don't have a clue how to handle a gun. Or what bullets they take, either."

Sighing, Devra realized that she didn't, either. Mom hated guns, and wouldn't allow any in the house. "Then let's go be vandals," she said.

Together, they left the shop, nervously checking the street. There was still no sign of life anywhere, neither human nor animal. It was very, very spooky. The girls kept together as they moved toward the parked cars.

A couple of them had their doors open, and one even had the motor running. But there was no sign of the owners in the street. Maybe they'd gone into one of the shops or something? Heather peered into each car as they passed them.

"Damn this town for being so backward," she muttered. "Not a car phone in sight."

Devra just watched their backs, trying to see anything that might be moving. But there was still nothing. And then she heard the sound of a baby crying from one of the stores up ahead. She gripped Heather's arm. "Listen!"

"I hear it," her friend said, with some relief. "There's somebody in there." It was the local bookstore. "Come on, maybe they know what's happening."

They hurried across the deserted street, and opened the door.

A snarling dog lunged for them. With a cry, Devra

threw herself backward. Heather let the door go, and it slammed into the dog's face as it jumped for them. Blurred images filled Devra's mind as she turned and stumbled back: the dog's twisted face, and saliva-dripping teeth; Heather's terrified features . . .

The people beyond the dog in the store, huddled together and terrified, with other dogs surrounding them . . .

Something slammed into the door, growling and snarling. Devra stopped thinking, and simply reacted. She whirled and ran, the frantic barking of the dogs behind her speeding her on. Heather managed to keep up with her.

"What's happening?" Heather gasped as she ran.

"Don't talk," Devra answered, stitch already starting to burn at her side. "We have to get somewhere safe."

It was only moments before they reached Devra's home. There was no sign of pursuit, but there was no telling how long that would last. Devra and Heather piled in, and they locked the door behind them.

As soon as she had sufficient breath, Devra called for her mother. There was no reply. Starting to breathe more normally, and with the stitch vanishing, Devra managed to start focusing her thoughts again. "Go around the house," she instructed. "Check that the doors and windows are all closed and locked. They may be after us soon."

"Dogs?" Heather said, as if she'd been hit in the head too hard. "Why would dogs come after us?"

"Why would they hold people captives in a bookstore?'' Devra yelled. ''How should I know? But they did it, and we don't have the time to try and figure it out. Check around.'' She started herself in the kitchen, and Heather went into the dining room. Together, it took them less than five minutes to secure the house as best they could. On the way around, Devra tried the phones, but they were all dead. She also called out for her mother several times, but without any response. Devra didn't want to try and imagine what might have happened to her.

Then she and Heather sat in the den, holding one another and shaking. All of their fears came to a peak, and they simply clutched at one another for physical and emotional support. But Heather couldn't stay quiet forever. She pulled free and looked at Devra.

''Is it just the dogs?'' she asked quietly. ''Have they formed packs, or something?''

''Don't forget the elephants,'' Devra replied. ''And that monkey, cutting the phone wires. It's like in Hitchcock's *The Birds,* only with all animals going mad.''

''That's the trouble, though,'' Heather pointed out. ''They're not really mad, are they? The dogs held those people *captive*. They seemed to have a purpose in mind. And the elephants closed the gates to stop people getting out. We might be the only free people left in town.''

''Free?'' Devra laughed bitterly, and waved her hand around. ''We're not free. It's just fear that's keeping us here.'' She took a deep breath. ''We have to think of something. I've been taking driver's ed—I think I could manage to drive us if we can find a car with keys in it.'

Mom's is in the garage right now, or I'd take that."

"Take it where?" asked Heather.

"For help, of course," Devra answered.

"*Is* there any help?" Heather demanded. "What if this isn't happening just here in Nolan? What if it's all over Florida? Or the country? Or the world?"

Devra hadn't thought of that. She'd just assumed that this was something local, that only the sleepy little town of Nolan was affected. The thought that this might be more widespread was even scarier. "We can't start imagining the worst!" she exclaimed. "It can't possibly be everywhere. It's got to be a problem here. Otherwise . . . otherwise, what hope is there?"

Heather nodded. "I guess. Well, that was just me being the pessimist. I'll try and be sunny and carefree from now on, okay?"

"Well, don't go to extremes." Devra stood up. "If we stay here, we can't help anyone. We have to find some way out of town. And pray that there is help out there for everyone. My mom is missing. And so is Ed. We can't just abandon them."

"No, we can't," Heather agreed. She seemed to be regaining her courage. "You're right, we have to try. We—" Abruptly, she gasped, and clutched at Devra's arm.

Devra whirled about and saw, in the doorway, that Spice was there, staring at them.

How could she have forgotten about her own dog? Had they locked themselves in the house with the enemy?

CHAPTER 6

COLONEL ADAIR FELT an immense sense of relief as he stared into the Contamination Room. The Black Death samples hadn't been touched at all. They were still in their protective vault, sealed and secure. He turned to Agent Parker, puzzled.

"I don't get it. Why would anybody break into a top security site like this, kill all the staff, and then take nothing? Unless something else is missing?"

The agent looked up from the computer console she was using. "According to the inventory log, there are only two items missing. The complete supply of an experimental drug named BZT and every single test animal on the island."

Adair scowled. "Maybe that means something to a highly educated person like yourself, ma'am," he said.

"But to a humble soldier like myself, it's crazy."

"You're not humble," she replied, a faint smile on her tight lips. "I've rarely met a man so full of himself."

That made him grin. "Well, I've got a whole lot of me to be full of. But you didn't answer my point."

For the first time, Parker looked really worried. "I've been formulating a theory," she admitted. "It sounds like something you'd expect from an agent named Mulder, though, not Parker."

"That whacked out, eh?" Adair shrugged. "Trust me, I've gone through most of the reasonable explanations I can think of. So try me with an unreasonable one."

"Okay." She took a breath. "I don't think we're investigating a break-in. I think we're investigating a break-out."

Adair didn't get it. "But there's nobody missing," he objected. "Surely you can't have forgotten we went through that room and identified every single corpse?"

Parker shuddered, looking human for once. "No. But there's nobody *human* missing."

Then he understood. "You think that the *animals* did this? But that's—"

"Unreasonable," she agreed. "Just what you asked for."

Adair's first impulse was to have her sent for a competency hearing. He stifled it, and considered her suggestion. "Aside from the fact that we don't appear to have any other suspects right now, do you have any evidence to back up your . . . idea?"

"Plenty." She started ticking the points off on her

fingers. "There's no sign of a landing anywhere on the island. No perimeter alarms were triggered, and not one guard was wounded or dead at his post. They were all brought *here* and then killed. The chances of twelve armed guards all being surprised from outside and captured without firing a shot is pretty remote. Unless they were taken from *within*. The bodies all show evidence of bites, most from small animals. Six of the men and two of the women were bitten to death. I'm not an animal expert, but I'd say most of those bites were from rabbits and rats. They're the correct size. And both were used here. There are just two animal corpses left behind, both of which died during drug testing. Every other animal has gone.

"Now, suppose for some reason some terrorist, paramilitary, or business group had found out about BZT testing and some miraculous effects it had. Something that was so great it would lead them somehow to come here and steal the whole supply. Why take the animals? The ones that BZT was tested on, maybe. But what about the animals in cancer research, or the other stuff? They wouldn't bother with them."

Adair nodded slowly. "Makes some kind of sense. Except that animals couldn't have done this." He waved his hand about the laboratory. "It's too well planned."

"And animals can't plan, right?" Parker sighed. "Actually, some can. *Science* published a report last year in which Brennon and Terrace of Columbia University proved that monkeys can count up to nine."

Adair snorted, good-humoredly. "I can just imagine

what you must do on your days off. But there's a long way from being able to count on your fingers—do you call them fingers in monkeys?—and committing mass murder. Mostly.''

"What I'm getting at is that monkeys are smarter than we probably think. Not smart enough to do this unaided, no. But that's where the BZT comes in. I checked the files, and three of the monkeys were being tested with it.''

"You think that the BZT somehow gave them smarts?'' Adair shook his head. "Maybe we should send some to every school cafeteria in the country.''

"I think it's possible,'' Parker said stubbornly. "And primates have opposable thumbs. They could open cages.''

Adair's mind was starting to work. What Parker was suggesting sounded absolutely crazy on the face of it. But it did fit the facts . . . and there was something else that occurred to him. "If the monkeys *were* made smarter, that still doesn't explain how they got the dumb animals to do as they were told. I mean, I had a pet rabbit once, and I couldn't even teach it to play fetch.''

Parker shook her head. "I know. Maybe my theory's just too far out.''

"Or maybe it's not far out enough.'' The colonel grinned. "Can you hack into the supply closet inventories from that thing?''

Parker actually cracked a genuine smile. "This is top of the line equipment,'' she answered. "I can even hack into Ted Turner's phone line, if you know his number.'' She started calling up data.

"Darn. I left it in my other suit. Check the inventory, and see how many syringes there are supposed to be. I'll check the closet itself.''

The scariest part was that the computer proved his craziest suspicions: more than two hundred syringes were missing. Adair stared at an almost empty box of hypodermics and shook his head. "The damn monkeys *did* become smart, Parker,'' he said slowly. "Then they started feeding the stuff to the other animals. They've *all* become smart. The question is—just how smart?''

"Too smart to hang around here,'' the agent answered. "There's a boat missing from the dock. Smart enough to pilot it, do you think?''

"No,'' Adair said with conviction. "They may be smart, but those boats are built for human-sized hands and weights. They'd never be able to turn the tiller. But—''

"But they could go with the tide,'' Parker finished for him. "Damn! That's why they struck when they did— to take advantage of the tides. But where would they end up?''

"Nolan,'' Adair answered. "Get ready to pull out. I'm calling in an evac. I better notify Halsey. Have him recon the town. We've got to get after those things. God knows what they'll do next. They're capable of planning and murder. . . .'' He shuddered. "Good work, Parker.''

She nodded. "Jayne,'' she offered.

Adair smiled. A breakthrough? "Thanks.'' He grabbed

the microphone that was slung over his back. "Adair to Mother Hen. The island is clear of hostiles. Send in an immediate clean-up crew. And an Osprey to get us moving. And find out where the tides would take a boat leaving the east dock here this morning."

General Halsey himself acknowledged. "Are we facing a terrorist threat?" he demanded.

Adair glanced at Parker. "Frankly, sir, we don't yet know. We're surely facing *something*, though." He briefed the general on their suspicions. "You might want to start moving troops into the area, though, to tell the truth, it might be hard catching our suspects."

"And why would that be, Colonel?" The general didn't like his men's abilities to be questioned.

"Because it's a bunch of rabbits and rats, sir. Oh, and a couple of monkeys." He explained quickly what Parker had guessed and then what they had discovered.

"That woman sounds like she's a few sandwiches short of a picnic," Halsey complained.

"Sir, I've been working with her all morning, and I find her to be a thoroughly professional and intelligent agent." That made her smile! Adair grinned back. "Which could, of course, mean I'm as crazy as she is."

"Ha!" Halsey snorted. "You've got your plane and the recovery team on the way. Also the securing force. They should be with you within ten minutes."

"And what about the tides, sir?" Adair insisted.

"They show that the boat would most likely have landed in a small town named Nolan. And, before you ask, we're trying to get through to the police there. But the phone lines seem to be down. These little pests of yours seem to be very intelligent."

"That they do. Adair, out." He replaced the microphone and then studied Agent Parker. "When it comes to stone faces, you could teach Mount Rushmore a thing or three. So—two words: what gives?"

Parker blinked once, slowly, before replying. "These animals took the BZT with them, Alan. They don't need it for themselves. . . ."

He understood what she was suggesting. "You think they've let it loose in Nolan?"

"I think that's what they intended it for, yes." She shivered. "Can you imagine what might be happening there? Three monkeys, a dozen rabbits, and half a hundred rats took out this entire facility. What would a town filled with intelligent, belligerent animals be capable of?"

Now he fully understood the look of horror on her face. Not just dozens, but possibly thousands of thinking, planning, hating creatures going after an unsuspecting town.

And just him and Jayne Parker going in to see if their worse nightmares might possibly have come true. . . .

CHAPTER 7

ED DIDN'T KNOW what to do. He stared from the wrong side of the bars out of the cage. One of the tigers was prowling slowly around, never taking his eyes from the crowded cage. Ed was certain he could read hatred in those flashing eyes, along with a strong desire to kill. And yet—the tiger hadn't killed. It was guarding the humans, fighting against its own nature and wishes. And that argued for some terrible level of intelligence. Animals very rarely went against their natures the way these beasts were doing.

There was something horribly wrong here. But he had no idea just how wrong. Were Heather and Devra safe? Was it just this zoo where things had gone contrary to nature? Or was this only one small island of madness in a sea of insanity? He *had* to get out of here, to find out what was happening. But how?

He looked around the other people in the cage. Most of them were young, either kids here while they had a few days left before school started, or mothers with kids. There were some men, off from work, who had come here with their families, but mostly the group was made up of younger children. And almost all of them were either silent and terrified, or crying hysterically. Either way, none of them could help. Celia *might* help, if she got her nerve together, but he wasn't sure he could rely on her. He wished he knew her better, knew whether she was the sort who might hold up under strain or the kind to crack and run sobbing to mommy.

The mothers were all, understandably, more worried about the safety of their kids than anything else. The men . . . he didn't know.

And then he saw that there was a young woman with the group. She was dressed in some kind of official uniform. Ed hadn't spotted this immediately, because it was smeared with mud and quite a lot of blood. Now he looked, he could see she had to be one of the keepers. He crossed the cage to join her. "Do you know what is happening?" he asked her.

She had been sitting, her face staring at the floor. She slowly looked up, and Ed tried to smile encouragingly. He failed miserably. She was quite pretty, and not much older than him. One of the college kids, home for the summer break, most likely, who'd taken a job at the game farm. Despite the blood splattered all over her, she didn't seem to be too injured. Just streaks on her arms and legs, and one small cut on her left cheek that had caked over.

"The world's turned upside down," she replied, in a flat, emotionless voice. "The captives are the captors, and those who looked in now look out."

Uh-oh. She didn't sound too well-hinged. "How did it happen?" he asked her gently. "What started it?"

"I don't know," she admitted. Her face was blank. "They turned on us, attacking us." She looked down at her blouse, and tapped the redness. "This is from Bryan. The tiger bit his head almost off. I thought it would kill me next, but it didn't." She rubbed her arms. "It just warned me, and made me come in here."

"How did the tiger get out?"

She looked at him. "The monkey let him out. The wise, crafty monkey stole Bryan's key and opened the door, letting out death and destruction. It bit him on the head, and I was showered in his blood."

Ed gave up. It was clear that she was in shock, having witnessed the murder of her friend and fearing she'd be next. She needed professional help, not to talk with him. "I'm sorry," he said to her. "I truly am. You rest, okay?"

Suddenly, she grinned at him, and bent forward. "They don't know I have a secret," she told him. Patting her blouse, she added: "I have the key in here. I had a spare, and they don't know there's a spare. But I have it." Her eyes were very wide, as if she were on drugs or something.

Ed was filled with hope. "You could get us out of here?" he asked, whispering with fierce intensity. He didn't want everyone to hear. It might start a riot.

"Oh, yes. I can get us out—into the jaws of death." She gestured carelessly at the prowling tiger.

"Yes," he agreed, deflated. "That is kind of a problem. Look, what's your name?"

"Anne."

"Okay, Anne. Do me a big favor." He smiled at her and patted her hand. "Don't tell anybody else about that key, okay? It's our secret, right?"

Anne nodded and tapped the side of her nose. "Mum's the word," she promised. Ed believed her. She was so out of it, it was unlikely anyone else would talk to her. He patted her again, and got to his feet. He always thought better when he was moving. He started to pace back and forth in the cage, trying to come up with something resembling, even slightly, a plan.

The only thing that immediately occurred to him was that he was behaving just like the former inhabitant of this cage—the tiger had always paced it like this. Had that been because he was trying to come up with a way out, too? Ed snorted. Maybe he and it weren't that far apart, after all. And, right now, their roles had certainly been reversed! He was inside the cage, and the tiger was outside watching them all.

How long had this been going on? He glanced at his watch and realized with a shock that it was only a little after one. It seemed as if the whole day must have passed by now, but he had only entered the zoo about two hours earlier. It was a long time till dark, and surely the animals out there would have to rest some time. That would be the best time to escape. Though tigers hunted at night, he recalled. Still, the tigers couldn't stay alert all day and then all night. They would have to sleep sometime. They were cats, after all, and cats tended to sleep a lot.

Ed drifted over to one of the cursing men. "If we can get that door open," he murmured, "are you interested in escape?"

"Interested? Of course I am!" The man glared at him. "I want to get home, get my guns, and come back here and shoot every last one of these disgusting creatures." His eyes narrowed. "Can you really get us out of here?"

"I hope so," Ed told him. "Look, talk to the others, and see who wants to try and make a break for it with us."

They split up. Ed went to Celia next and asked her the same question. She stared out of the cage at the tiger, her eyes dilated in fear.

"They'll kill us if we try," she said, her voice shaking. "I can't do it."

"Would you rather stay in here?" Ed asked. He felt both pity and contempt for the girl. He supposed he shouldn't really blame her, but she was nothing like either Devra or Heather. "You don't know what they have in mind for us."

"They're just animals," Celia protested. "And somebody will be along to kill them and rescue us soon."

"Optimist," Ed muttered. He wasn't so sure of that. There had been plenty of time by now for the girls to have contacted the police, even if they'd had to run to the station house. If help was coming, they should have heard sirens and gunfire by now. The silence said it all. Still, since there was no point in talking to Celia further, he moved on to one of the mothers with a young boy and tried her next.

"I'm hungry," the boy complained. "When are we going to eat?"

"I don't know, sweetheart," the mother answered, worried. "There's nothing in this cage to eat at all."

That was something that Ed hadn't considered. He'd eaten his hot dog and fries just before the attack, so he was okay for a while. But there was no food or water in here, except for the tiger's water bowl. That wouldn't last the crowd here very long, even if people could bring themselves to sip from it. Did the animals intend them to dehydrate or starve? Or would they bring food?

In the end, only four other people wanted to try a break with Ed and the first man. The rest all preferred to wait for "rescue."

"Idiots," the cursing man snorted. "There's nobody coming in the near future. How long do they want to wait? It already stinks in here because of the kids urinating. And it's going to get much worse."

Another good point. Ed sighed. "I was thinking it might be best to wait until dark."

"Some of those animals have excellent night vision," one of the women objected. "They'll probably be on guard after dark. The bats, maybe." She shuddered.

"I've always had nightmares about being attacked by bats."

That was a point Ed hadn't considered. "Twilight, then. The bats will just be waking up, and the tigers and deer should be getting really sleepy. If we stick together as a group, we should be able to fight off whoever tries to come after us. If we can get to one of the buildings or the cars, we should be able to stand a better chance. There have to be guns in the administration building."

"Good," the first man said. "I want to blow these critters straight to hell."

One of the mothers pointed out of the cage. "Something's happening!" she called.

Everyone turned to look. Ed saw that a monkey had come down from the trees and was scuttling along the ground toward the cage. The deer and even the tiger moved aside to let it through. It stopped outside the cage, at a safe distance, and stared at the humans within. Ed saw that it was a female, and there was cunning in her eyes.

It's feeding time.

The voice wasn't aloud. Ed jerked, realizing he'd heard it directly in his mind. The *monkey* had said that! He would have been more astonished if his brain hadn't been so worn down by the events of the day.

"The damn thing can *talk!*" the cursing man exclaimed in disbelief. The crowd started to argue amongst themselves. Obviously, everybody had heard the voice.

One of the mothers with a young child moved forward, hesitantly, looking at the monkey. "You're going to feed us?'' she asked, timidly, flushing, as if what she was doing was foolish. ''My baby is starving.''

You don't understand, the monkey's voice said coldly. *You're not getting fed—he is.* The monkey gestured at the tiger. *And he eats only fresh meat.*

A wave of ice ran through Ed's body as he understood what the creature was saying. He felt sickened and scared. ''You can't feed one of *us* to him!'' he blurted out.

The monkey stared at him. *We can't feed one of* us *to him any longer,* he pointed out. *We are now all one brotherhood. So it must be one of you. Besides, after all of these years that you slaughtered animals for your meals . . . it's time for payback.*

There was a howl of protest and fear over this comment. The first man stepped forward, his fists clenched. ''You filthy creatures!'' he yelled. ''You're going to pay for this, all of you!''

I am not interested in your views, the monkey replied. She glanced at the tiger. *You may choose your meal now.*

The tiger stepped forward. Ed felt another shiver of terror as the green eyes swept over him. There was a whimper from beside him, and his arms instinctively went around Celia Cameron, and she clung to him for comfort and protection, as if there was anything he could do right now but hold her! The crowd had gone absolutely silent, each person—even the babies, somehow—knowing that their lives were on the line.

This one.

The monkey's voice had sounded almost human, but

the tiger's was very, very different. It was like the roar
of thunder, or the flash of lightning against a totally dark
sky. An elemental force, something impossible to speak
back to or dare to argue with.

Ed felt ashamed at the relief that flooded through him.
The tiger had picked the cursing man, the one who
wanted to come back and wipe out all of the animals.
Celia gasped in relief, too, but she didn't let go of him.

"No!" the man screamed, backing away. The crowd
parted behind him, leaving him exposed to the gaze of
the animals. "You can't do it! I won't do it!"

The monkey opened the cage door. *Come out and run
for it.*

"No!" The man turned to the others in the cage.
"Don't let them take me! Please!"

Come out, the tiger demanded. *Or I shall come in and
take you. And if I do, other people may be hurt.*

That threat produced results—probably the one in-
tended. Several of the mothers pushed the man away.
"Go!" one woman screamed. "You can't risk us all!
Go!"

"No," the man whimpered. His defiant spirit had broken completely when he had heard the strength and
power in the tiger's voice. "I can't!"

Two of the other men started forward, grabbing hold
of him. Ed was horrified and sickened that the others
should have turned on the man so easily. And he was
ashamed that he stood by and watched. But he couldn't
bring himself to move. The two men dragged the screaming, pleading target to the cage door, and flung him out-

side. They looked relieved when the monkey locked the cage door.

Run! the creature commanded. *Perhaps you can escape . . .*

As if . . . Ed shook his head. The tiger wanted the joy of a kill as it ran, not one that stood and shook, and the monkey was giving it that. The man whimpered, and then turned and ran.

The tiger waited, its tail flicking, its eyes burning. The man vanished into the bushes, and then the tiger uncoiled. It sprang into fluid motion, throwing itself down the pathway after its target. Ed held his breath as he held Celia tight. It was as much comfort for himself as it was for her.

There was a scream, which abruptly turned to a gurgle, and then into silence. The tiger roared, and then there was the sound of bones breaking.

Ed gagged. Celia couldn't stop herself from vomiting. Several of the others in the cage did the same. It didn't improve the stench.

The monkey turned to stare at them all again. *That is all you humans are good for,* it informed them. *You are food, nothing else. One by one, you will be devoured.* It paused, and then added: *Have a nice day.* Then it turned and made its way across to one of the other cages.

Celia had managed to wipe her mouth with a tissue. She was looking younger, terrified, her eyes red, her nose running. Ed felt horribly sorry for her. And just as sorry for himself. "So," he asked grimly, "do you still want to wait here to be rescued?"

"No," she said, softly. "Anything is better than what happened to that poor man. Even if they kill us, I'm coming with you when you escape."

"Good girl." He ruffled her hair. "Don't take this the wrong way, but—you *really* need a bath."

"If we get out of here," she vowed, "I'm spending a week scrubbing myself clean."

If we get out of here . . . Ed knew that was the problem. *Could* they escape before they were slated for a tiger's dinner?

CHAPTER 8

EVRA STARED AT her pet, for the first time in her life feeling fear when she saw Spice. Was the dog here to turn on her, like the other animals had done? Were she and Heather trapped in the house with the enemy? "Spice," she said slowly, hoping this made some sort of sense to her pet, "are you still my best girl?"

Spice cocked her head on one side. *Of course I am, silly.*

Stunned, Devra's eyes widened as she tried to think about what she had just heard. She looked at Heather, and saw the same bewildered look on her face. "You heard her, too?" Her friend nodded weakly.

It's something new, Spice said briskly. *It started this morning. All of a sudden I could think more clearly, and see things differently. It's been fun exploring everywhere. And then I discovered I could talk to everyone!* Her tongue lolled out of her mouth. *Isn't this fun? Now I can tell you when I want something, instead of having to play stupid charades with you all of the time.*

Devra had to sit down, as she tried to take all of this in. Heather collapsed onto the carpet next to her. Spice ambled over, and licked at Devra's hand. Automatically, she scratched the back of the dog's head.

Oh yessss! Spice said, ecstatically. *More!*

Devra kept going, not daring to stop. "This all happened today?" she asked. "You started to get smarter? And then you could talk? Talk to who?"

Oh, everybody, Spice explained. *Other dogs. Cats. Even the birds. And the monkey.*

"What monkey?" asked Devra, suspicion dawning in her. Could it be the same one she'd seen at the game farm?

The one that hates people, Spice replied. *She wanted us all to capture or kill all of the people in town. Me, I don't care what happens to everybody else, but I love you, Devra. I wouldn't hurt you. You've been really good to me. And I'll make sure nobody else hurts you, either.*

"And what about me?" Heather asked anxiously.

Spice obviously had to think about that. *You're okay,* she finally decided. *You always liked to scratch me, too. And you gave me treats . . . sometimes. You can hang around for now.*

"Gee, thanks," muttered Heather.

Devra stopped scratching Spice. "But what can we do

now?'' she asked. ''What happened to Mom?''

Spice shrugged mentally. *No idea. I hope she's okay. She went out earlier somewhere, and hasn't come back.*

Devra's stomach churned. Mom was out somewhere, possibly in danger from these creatures. And Ed certainly was in danger, along with everyone else in the game farm. The monkey seemed to be the ringleader of this revolt, and it hated people. She didn't know why, and she hoped she'd never find out. ''There are a lot of people in trouble,'' she said. ''We have to try and help them.''

Oh, no! Spice said firmly. *To help humans, I'd have to turn on my fellow animals, and I would never do that. I'll look after the two of you, but that's it. The rest of them can fend for themselves.*

''They might not be able to!'' Devra exclaimed.

Tough, Spice said unsympathetically. *I've no great love for humans in general. Not after what happened to me. Only you cared, Devra, and looked after me. That's why I'm looking after you now.* Spice stood up and headed toward the door. *Come on, we have to get out of here.*

''Why?'' asked Heather. ''We're safe in here.''

Safe? Spice gave a scornful laugh. *Do you think the other animals don't know you're here? They'll be after you soon. There's only one thing we can do. We have to go to see the monkey and plead your case.*

''Is that safe?'' Devra asked, shocked.

No, Spice admitted. *But if the monkey wants you dead, it will happen. I have to sleep some time, and there are a lot of animals who'd gladly kill you. Most of them have absolutely no love for human beings. Not like me.*

"You're a good girl, Spice," Devra said sincerely. She had never dreamed that saving Spice's life as she had would ever be paid back in kind. "I guess you're right. We really don't have any choice."

Oh, and the name's not "Spice" anymore, the dog added. *It doesn't really suit me. I'm going to be known from now on as Proud Huntress of the Night. But you can call me Huntress.*

"Gee, thanks," said Devra. As if Spice had ever hunted anything other than an opened can of dog food or a squeaky toy! But this wasn't the time or place to argue, that was for sure. Not when they needed her help so badly. Devra opened the door.

Six dogs were there, waiting, their teeth bared.

She gasped, and jumped back. Spice stepped forward.

Knock it off, guys! she snapped. *These two are with me. Nobody is going to hurt my pets.*

Pets? Devra stared at the animals in shock. Spice— er, Huntress—thought that *she* was the pet? Devra was incredibly humiliated by that.

I don't think we're allowed pets, a mastiff complained. *Nobody told me I could have a pet!*

Right, agreed a poodle. *We're supposed to herd the humans, or kill them. Not adopt them as pets just because they followed us home.*

I don't care, Spice/Huntress said with a sniff. *These two are my pets, and you're not going to hurt them.*

I don't know about that, the mastiff complained.

Look, Huntress snapped. *I'm taking them to the monkey, Penelope, in the game farm. I'm going to plead my case there. Why don't you come along, and see what she says? Maybe she'll think it's a great idea, and let you all have pets.*

That sounds cool, agreed a border collie. *I'd like to have a pet to throw my toys, and scratch me. I can't quite get the back of my head just right.*

Devra gave Heather a glare, and her friend caught on. "Here," she said, stepping forward. "Let me." She scratched at the itchy spot.

You know, the collie said, *I think you've got a point, Huntress. Maybe we do need pets.*

Okay, the poodle said with a sigh. *It looks like we'd better get a decision on this. I can do without pets myself, but some of you weaker souls might need them.*

Their lives had been saved for now, Devra realized, but they hadn't yet been assured. What would this monkey, Penelope, say? She seemed to have a hatred for human beings for some reason. Was she likely to agree to the dogs keeping her and Heather alive?

And worse—were the two of them now completely dependent on making dogs happy to stay alive? Would they be forced to become slaves to animals that had once been devoted to them in order to prolong their own lives? And, if so, would the humiliation be worth it? Devra didn't know. All she knew was that this was a nightmare she wished she could waken from. But she strongly suspected that she couldn't.

Slowly, the small procession walked through the

streets of Nolan. It had only been a couple of hours ago that Devra's worst problem was deciding what to do with the day. Now she didn't even know if she would survive it.

The dogs were behaving oddly. They were still dogs, and as a result kept getting distracted by sniffing bouts at trees and so forth. They would even lope off and play from time to time. But they were also clearly more intelligent now, and there was always at least one pair of doggie eyes on Devra and Heather. They were not trusted, that was clear.

And, come to think of it, why should they be? She had always loved and taken care of her pets, but this wasn't true of everyone. Some people bought dogs to chain them up as guards. Others bought them to fight for money. Many kids teased family pets cruelly. And some, like Huntress's previous owners, simply abandoned them when they became inconvenient. On the whole, the human race had a fairly lousy track record with pets.

And what about non-pets? Squirrels, rats, raccoons . . . many were trapped and killed by people. As for cows, sheep, or pigs . . . they were doomed to be eaten. Even animals like tigers were hunted and killed, and many were simply callously displaced when humans wanted their lands. And it was all done because humans *could* do it. They had the power, the brains, to be able to do this to animals.

But not, it appeared, anymore. Just how widespread was this problem? Only in Nolan? The whole state? The entire country?

The world?

Maybe she could get some information from the dogs. They seemed to be very talkative, at least amongst themselves. Maybe they'd tell her what they knew. Of course, the problem was whether they knew very much at all.

Devra realized she was clutching Heather's hand for support. She squeezed it, and then managed to put a smile on her face. "Do you know how this all started?" she asked the dogs. "I mean, one or two of you must have heard talk."

It was the right approach. The poodle snorted. *Of course we know,* it replied loftily. *We're not ignorant humans. It started with Penelope.*

She was in a testing laboratory, the border collie answered. *There was a new drug there that made her smarter, and enabled her to talk like this. She gave it to the other animals there, and they all became smarter, too.*

They'd all been hurt by the humans, the mastiff added darkly. *So they got their revenge, and killed the killers. Then they came here with more of their drug.*

"They must be talking about Cobra Island," Heather said suddenly. "There's some sort of bio-engineering going on there. They must have developed something."

Right, agreed Huntress. *And Penelope came here and put it into the town water supply, so all of the animals drank it in. And then we all became smart, too.*

"But we humans drank the water," objected Devra. "It hasn't changed us."

How could it? snorted the mastiff. *It's given us human intelligence. You already have that.*

"And this telepathy stuff," Heather added. "And we didn't get that. Did we?" She screwed up her face and stared at Devra. "You didn't get my thought?"

"Not a word," admitted Devra. "Maybe the drug only works on animals."

Whatever, Huntress said. *At any rate, we've all become a whole lot smarter. And now humans can't do as they want with us anymore. The tables have turned, and we're in charge.*

The only thing you humans had going for yourselves was your brain, the mastiff added. *And now we're on your level. But we have other things you don't have—stronger teeth, faster bodies, more powerful claws . . .*

"But we have guns and stuff," Heather objected.

Only when you get to use them, the collie replied. *And we're smart enough not to let that happen now.*

Devra realized that the dogs were right. Humans' only advantage now was to strike first. But nobody outside of town knew what was happening. "It's just Nolan that's affected so far," she realized. "That's it."

It has to start somewhere, the mastiff said. *Once we have control here, we can go on and free the rest of the animals.*

"Oh, great," muttered Heather. "They're all *today Nolan—tomorrow the world* nuts!"

The mastiff glared up at her. *There are more animals than humans in this world,* he informed her coldly. *Now we're making certain that we're not going to be forced out of it just because of what humans want. It's going to be a whole new world from now on. One in which humans don't rule.*

It could happen, Devra realized. As far as she knew, nobody had the slightest idea outside of town that there was anything wrong. And by the time they did, the animals would be on the move. Even if somebody found out, the human race could hardly stop it spreading, unless . . .

"This drug that the monkey brought," she said. "She's got to be running out of it. And it's not something animals can make, is it? So you *can't* spread out. There will only be the few of you here in town that are smart. The others will stay the way they are."

No, Huntress said. *It's not like that. Penelope knows how to make more of the drug. She said so.*

"And you believe her?" asked Devra.

Why would she lie to us? asked the collie, confused.

"How about because she wanted to get you to turn on the humans, thinking this was the start of a war?" suggested Heather. "When all it is is a tiny little jail break?"

That's not it at all! the poodle protested.

"Well, we'll soon find out," Devra said grimly. They had reached the gates of the sealed game farm. "We're here." She banged on the gate, and felt the confusion from the other side.

Who's there? Demanded a slow, ponderous voice. It had to be one of the elephants.

"One of the former masters of the Earth," Devra said

bitterly. "We've come to see Penelope and to plead our case. You'd better let us in. We're with friends of yours."

The gate swung slightly open, as the elephant tugged at it with his trunk. It gave Devra, Heather, and the dogs just enough room to squeeze in. The elephant stared at the girls in confusion.

Just let us pass, Huntress snapped. *We have to talk with Penelope. It's important for all of us!*

The elephant considered a moment, and then moved aside. Devra swallowed as she walked past it. She tried to look and sound brave, but she knew that she and Heather might be marching to their deaths. So Huntress was on their side, and the other dogs weren't exactly opposed. They weren't the real foes here. The ones she had to fear most were waiting ahead.

" 'Won't you come into my lair, said the spider to the fly,' " she quoted. "I've got a bad feeling about this."

"You have?" Heather was almost white. "I want a bathroom."

"You should have gone before we left," Devra replied.

Go on one of the bushes, the poodle suggested. *Nobody will object. We're not humans.*

"No thanks," Heather said. "I'll wait."

Suit yourself. The poodle lost interest in her, sniffing at the bushes herself. *Hey, there's lots of good stuff here!*

They walked on. Devra shuddered as she saw bones smashed and scattered across the path. Blood was still congealing. She didn't want to think about what had happened here. Or even what lay ahead.

Was there any chance that she and Heather could survive this? Any at all?

CHAPTER 9

COLONEL ADAIR SHIFTED in his seat in the Osprey, staring at the video screen. General Halsey stared back, looking very, very worried. As he should be. The air reconaissance mission had reported its findings. The situation was bad, but it looked like it was going to get much, much worse.

"The town of Nolan appears to be completely cut off," the general reported. "About five miles in all directions, there's no contact at all. Then everything's fine. I've ordered the roads closed and blocked by the police for now."

"Fine," Adair answered. "Now, you have to get troops in. Surround the place, and let *nothing* through. Not an animal, not a bird. I think we'd be safe with insects. Either trap or kill anything else that tries to leave."

"And how are we to do that?" demanded Halsey. "We're used to fighting men, damn it, not animals."

"In a word," Adair answered: "flamethrowers. Burn out an area about a hundred yards across, so the troops can see anything attempting to cross it. I don't know if what they'll find will be intelligent animals or not, but Cobra Island proves they mean business. We have no choice here. Trap them, kill them, or fry them. But if you let them out, we'll be in serious trouble."

Parker was looking at him with obvious approval for his plans. He didn't need her approval, of course, but it felt good to have it. He'd come to respect her in a very short while. She was a remarkably competent person.

"Though that may not be enough," she added.

"I agree," Adair said. She'd thought this through, as he had suspected she would. He turned back to the screen. "General, your intelligence reports indicate that for the moment this problem is confined to Nolan. We have to keep it that way. Once we go in, give us two hours. If we don't contact you with positive news by that point—destroy the town. Level it. Leave nothing alive."

There was a slight pause, and Halsey looked troubled. "Damn it, Alan you're talking about murdering innocent civilians."

"I know what I'm talking about," Adair said calmly. "Killing anyone in Nolan that the animals haven't beaten us to. But we simply can't chance any of those smart animals getting loose. Some of them may be burrowers, and if birds are affected, some of them may be able to get away. Also, we're not sure that human survivors might not be carriers."

Halsey scowled. "What do you think, Agent Parker?" he asked, as if seeking a way out.

Parker nodded her head. "I agree completely with Colonel Adair's recommendation, sir. Killing a few thousand innocent civilians might save millions later."

The general hesitated and then nodded. "Two hours," he agreed. "That should give us time to concoct a plausible cover story if we have to take out the town." He coughed. "Good luck to you both. I hope to God we don't have to kill you."

"Trust me, sir," Adair answered with a grin, "I'll do everything I can to make that move unnecessary." He clicked off the comm unit and turned to face Parker.

"Can he manage to take out the town cleanly?" she asked, worried. "I mean, so that *nothing* can survive?"

"Yes," Adair assured her. "We've got tactical nuclear warheads that can take out a five-mile radius with very little fallout. One of those would do the trick. Then some story about Arab terrorists, or a gas line explosion or something will hide the truth." He looked at her seriously. "Your job is over, Parker. You don't have to come in with me. Risking my life alone is enough."

"I was assigned to this case, Adair," she replied. "You don't have the authority to take me off it. I'm coming along."

He nodded. "I kind of thought you'd say that. And I'm glad. You're a smart cookie."

"That sounds like sexual harassment to me, Colonel," Parker said sternly. Then she smiled slightly. "But thanks for the compliment."

Adair grunted, and finished suiting up again. No need for a wet suit this time, so he and she were both dressed in fatigues. He had the radio on his back again, and this time had a string of grenades, his pistol, his knife, and a heavy-duty rifle. Parker watched him kit up.

"No elephant rifle?" she asked. "I thought you preferred quiet and cunning?"

"Now that we know what we're up against, I prefer firepower," he admitted. "Anything that moves is a potential enemy, and I aim to get them first."

Parker sighed. "Has it occurred to you that we might be able to talk to them?"

Adair shook his head. "Two words: Cobra Island."

"Look, I know it was bad there, Alan," she admitted. "But you have to try and see it from their point of view. Those animals there were experimental subjects. Many were in pain. Most of them would die. The animals had no love for those humans."

"And why would they have love for *any* humans?" Adair argued.

"They may not have," Parker agreed. "But, by the same token, they don't necessarily hate all the human race. They may not have killed the people of Nolan."

Adair considered her point. "Tell you what," he said. "I'm not real good at negotiations. My idea of talking with a terrorist is to do it with a gun to his head— whether they're human or not. But if the animals haven't tried a wholesale massacre of the Nolanites, then I'll let you try to talk to them. Either way, we've got two hours to be in and out, or else we'll be in and toast." He grinned. "And I was kind of hoping I could take you out to dinner afterward, so I'd prefer not to get charred."

Parker smiled back. "Funny, I was going to ask you to dinner. As long as we don't have to kill and cook it ourselves."

"Boy, you sure know how to take the fun out of dining out," Adair pretended to complain. He loaded plenty of extra ammunition in his pack, and closed everything up. "Maybe you'd better take a little extra firepower along with you this time."

"I might be more dangerous to us than to any targets with that kind of a cannon," she admitted. "I've got plenty of spare bullets, and I know how to use my pistol, thanks."

"Grenades?" he suggested, tapping a box with his foot.

"How thoughtful." Parker helped herself to several. "How long is the delay?"

"Five seconds. You *can* count that high?"

She grinned fully this time. "Hey, even monkeys can, remember? Well, I guess I'm as ready as I'll ever be. How much longer?"

Adair glanced at the instruments. "Any time we like. These guys have been circling, to give us the time to prepare." He tapped the pilot on the shoulder. When the man looked around, Adair gestured downward. "Take us in."

"Yes, sir."

The hum of the engines changed pitch. Adair gestured for Parker to look out of the window. This time, they could watch as the Osprey's engines moved from horizontal to vertical. Their forward motion slowed, and they began to hover instead. The pilot took the airplane down, landing lightly.

"Ground floor," he called out. "Ladies' lingerie, terrorists and bombs."

"Sounds good to me," Adair answered, opening the door. "As soon as we're clear, get out of here."

"Good luck," the pilot called.

"I suspect we're going to need it," Parker muttered. She followed Adair out, and the door slammed and locked behind them.

They were on a small beach, with rocks scattered about. A long, narrow jetty stuck out into the sea, with a couple of boats bobbing up and down. Aside from the aircraft on the sands, it looked quite normal here. Adair started to run toward the road that paralleled the beach. There were no cars moving, no sign of people and no animals. Not even a seagull trawling for scraps. Behind them, the Osprey lifted off and moved out to sea, to take up its position. Either it would be back for them in two hours, or it would monitor the destruction of the entire area.

Two hours. Not much time. He wasn't looking forward to what he would find. It was a nice day, and there should have been at least a few people on this beach.

They made it to the road. The first houses lay on the opposite side. About a quarter of a mile up the road were the start of other roads and shops. Nolan was a sleepy town, but there should have been some signs of activity. There were none.

"Should we check out the houses?" Parker asked. Adair could hear the strain in her voice. He couldn't blame her for it. He managed to stay calmer because this was his normal working experience—laying his life on the line to face unknown dangers. She was probably more used to tracking counterfeiters or bank robbers. Rough work, but not with a two-hour limit on your life.

"It would take too long," he answered. "Let's try the shops down the road. Even in this hick town, there should be shopkeepers there all day."

"Makes sense," she agreed.

They moved cautiously. Adair scanned for signs of anything at all moving. Right now even a rat could be considered dangerous. But there was nothing. They reached the first store, and he gestured for Parker to hold back. "Cover me," he murmured, swinging his rifle into place for rapid firing, just in case.

Then he kicked open the door.

It was an ice cream store. Should be buzzing on a day like this. But there was nobody there at all. One of the tables lay on its side, and there were pools of melted ice cream all over.

"Everybody's gone," he reported. "It's like the audience for a Pauly Shore movie. Not a good sign."

"But no blood," Parker pointed out. "So no victims, either."

A good point. They tried the next store, a small convenience store. Once again, there were signs that people had been there and left in a hurry. Only this time they found blood. Parker examined it quickly.

"Human," she decided. "Too much blood, I'd say, for a routine accident. Maybe it's an animal bite. Hard to tell. If it *was* a bite, it was not big enough to kill."

They moved out again, and Parker touched his arm. "Listen."

He paused, and heard what her ears had caught first: a baby's cry. "Jackpot," he murmured. "The first time in my life I've been glad of a badly behaved kid. Better be ready for trouble."

Parker nodded. "Since there are people alive, I get to try talking," she pointed out.

"I remember. Let's hope these beasts speak English, kid." He followed the sound of the baby, and came to a small two-story building that was the local library. "Checkout time," he said with a grin. He slung the rifle back over his shoulder and slipped his pistol from its holster. Indoors, the rifle would be too unwieldy. "Ready?" At her nod, he opened the door.

A German shepherd leaped for him, teeth flashing. Adair didn't even think; he simply shot it three times. The dead animal crashed to the floor, and he vaulted the carcass. There were other dogs behind it, and lots of people in the body of the building.

"I'm assuming you fellows are smart," Adair called out as several more dogs moved toward him and Parker. "So *be* smart." He showed them the pistol. "I'm a very good shot, and there's no need to force me to kill you."

The dogs froze in place. So they *could* understand! That made things a whole lot easier.

"Kill them!" one woman screamed hysterically. "Kill them all, quickly! They've kept us prisoners!"

"Well, that's one vote for mayhem and murder," Adair said, watching the dogs closely and keeping his pistol leveled. "Any against?"

Humans! came a scornful voice in his mind. *Always that love of killing.*

It took all of Adair's self-control not to let his guard down at that moment. *They were able to talk through some form of telepathy!* Adair saw from the corner of his eye the shock on Parker's face. "Well, guys," he managed to reply, gesturing at the dead shepherd, "this fellow started it. I just hate to lose arguments. Now, do I continue shooting you, or do we talk?"

The dogs stared at one another, and then a spaniel stepped forward. *There is nothing that you can say that would interest us,* he replied.

"Oh, I don't know," Adair said. "How about listening for a moment, Fido?"

My name isn't Fido, the dog snapped. *It's Champion Lochinvar Grey.*

"Wow, royalty." Adair shook his head. "Okay, Champ, are you going to listen, or do you prefer to go to that great glue factory in the sky?"

"Your negotiating skills leave something to be desired," Parker commented.

"Told you so," Adair agreed amicably. "You have a go then."

Parker stepped forward. "We humans know what's going on here," she said. "You will never be allowed to leave Nolan. There are troops surrounding the town with orders to shoot any animals that try and leave."

You're lying, the spaniel said.

"Hey, it's easy to prove," Adair snapped. "Go for walkies and get shot."

"Adair!" Parker hissed. "Leave this to me." She stepped forward again. "I know why you're doing this, but it's not the answer. We need to talk." She smiled. "Take me to your leader." She turned back to Adair. "I've wanted to say that ever since I was a little girl," she confessed.

"I'm glad your childhood ambition has been reached," he answered.

The dogs conferred amongst themselves for a moment. Finally, the spaniel turned back to face them.

Very well, he agreed. *But these humans will remain here with us. They are our prisoners, and will not be freed unless we decide upon it.*

"No!" one of the men called. "You've got to get us out of here! We've had no food or water all day. They're trying to kill us! Get them first!"

"I'm sorry, sir," Parker replied. "This is currently a hostage situation. I'm sure there are more people being held elsewhere. We have to consider them. We'll try and get the animals to free you shortly."

"In just under an hour and forty minutes," Adair muttered. "Time's running out."

"I know," Parker agreed. She watched as a Scottish terrier stepped forward.

I'll take you to Penelope, she said. *Come with me.*

"Great," muttered Adair. "We get the dog with the shortest legs just when we're in a hurry."

The captives all tried begging for help, but Adair had to steel his heart. These people were in pain and anguish, but he had to consider the larger picture right now. Hopefully, they'd be free soon.

Or they'd be dead.

CHAPTER 10

THE TROOPS BEGAN to spread out as ordered by their commanding officers. In the forefront were the men with the flamethrowers. None of them had been told why they were doing this, of course; there was no need for them to know *why,* just to follow orders. No matter how strange those orders were.

General Halsey watched them from his command vehicle. He could have stayed behind in Washington, of course, but what kind of a general fights from the rear? He wanted to be on the scene, able to see and judge the situation for himself. And, if he was honest with himself, to look Nolan in the eye if he was forced to nuke it. It would have been cowardice to do otherwise. If he was going to have the blood of five thousand civilians—plus one extremely good soldier and an FBI agent—on his hands, he wanted to *see* the result of his orders, not to hide behind the walls of the Pentagon.

The flamethrowers roared to life, and the men began clearing away swaths of growth, mostly scrub bushes and small trees. The problem, then, wouldn't be clearing the buffer zone, but preventing the fires they started from spreading. The men were doing their best to go with the prevailing winds, but Halsey had a number of fire trucks standing by, in case they should be needed.

As far as anyone knew, this was just a military exercise. The troops were ordered to kill any animals that crossed the burned zone—trapping them would prove too unreliable and time-consuming—and Halsey didn't care what the men thought of his orders. They might think him mad, or that this was simply a test of how accurate their marksmanship was. Or they might just think this whole thing was some political nonsense. He didn't know and he didn't care. All he worried about was that they do their job.

And all he prayed was that Adair would call in before the deadline and call off the strike.

But he had to be ready for it, and he would be. The Air Force was flying in a T-12 missile, and it would be in place thirty minutes before the strike. It would take out Nolan in one incandescent moment if it had to. Halsey hoped fervently that he would not have to order its use. But Halsey was a man who understood his duty. If he had to destroy the town, he would.

And he'd be haunted by the act the rest of his life.

*   *   *

Ed had managed to settle down for the moment in the cage. There was nothing to lean against but the bars, and they hurt his back after a while. He'd allowed Celia to lean against him, so she'd at least get some comfort. In other circumstances, he'd have enjoyed having a pretty girl like her huddled up next to him. But these weren't other circumstances.

These were a nightmare.

The tiger had ambled back after its kill, and then collapsed, sleeping, on the pathway outside the cage. Ed vaguely recalled that the big cats tended to be drowsy after a kill—which was undoubtedly the reason the other two tigers hadn't yet eaten. They were now smart enough to know they should take this in rotation, so there would be two of them awake at all times.

That would make escape a lot harder. But he couldn't simply stay in the cage and await his turn to be tiger food. He was getting hungry himself, and so was everyone else in the cage. Not to mention thirsty. He was trying to avoid thinking about that. Everybody had been forced to drink a little from the tiger's bowl, but it was now empty, and the animals showed no interest in refilling it. Well, why should they bother looking after their human captives, only to feed them to the tigers and bears later?

How could this have happened? Ed didn't know. Somehow, the animals had had their intelligences boosted. They were all now roughly on a par with men. And, unsuspected, they had obviously struck the keepers and freed themselves. It was appalling to imagine animals having the same minds as men. They would not be safe, ever again.

He had to get out of here. He was willing to chance being hunted by the tigers. At least that would be a fast death. Waiting here to be taken would be a slower, more painful one.

"I'm hungry," Celia complained, echoing most of the children. Many of the younger ones had fallen asleep, thankfully. But those that hadn't were scared and whining. Like, in fact, Celia herself. She might be a teenager, but she was acting like a child right now.

"We're all hungry," Ed pointed out. "But there's nothing to eat. The animals won't feed us."

"Selfish jerks!" Celia screamed, grabbing hold of the bars. "I fed you often enough! I bought the food cups, and you ate from my hands! Can't you even return the favor, you selfish creeps?"

"I don't think they're listening," Ed said, gently. He wasn't sure what to do with Celia. She seemed to be on the verge of a breakdown.

"You're right," she agreed, shaking her fist at the placid deer. She settled back against his side. "And I have to go to the bathroom. And I'm *filthy*. I want a shower, a meal, and a bed. I *don't* want to be here."

"We'll get out," he promised her. "As soon as twilight falls, we'll make a break for it."

"If that stupid girl really does have a key," Celia complained. "Did you see it?"

"No," he admitted. "She said she'd hidden it inside

her blouse, and I didn't think it was polite to ask to look.''

''Polite?'' Celia laughed sharply. ''Who cares about polite? This is *survival* we're talking about.'' She jumped to her feet. Alarmed, Ed followed her as she headed for Anne, the keeper.

''She's not all there,'' he warned Celia. ''She may be vague. You have to be gentle.''

''Forget gentle,'' the girl snarled. ''I'm ready to try ballistic.'' She reached Anne. ''You! Where's this key you say you've got?''

The keeper looked up, her eyes vacant, her face dreamy. She smelled badly of blood and other fluids. ''The key to our minds,'' she murmured, ''is in our thoughts. And our little brethren out there have joined us.''

''And I'm about ready to take you apart,'' Celia snarled. ''Show me the key, you moron!''

Anne tapped her head. ''The key is our thoughts,'' she repeated.

''She doesn't have any stupid key!'' Celia yelled, furious. ''She's just imagining it!''

Ed slapped his hand over Celia's mouth. ''Keep your voice down, you idiot! Remember, those animals understand English! If they hear you, we're in trouble.''

''Over a nonexistent key?'' Celia mumbled. She whirled on Anne again. ''You stupid cow! You got all of our hopes up over nothing!'' She grabbed hold of the keeper's shoulders and started to shake her in fury.

His stomach twisting in frustration and disappointment, Ed stood watching for a second. He had placed so much hope on that key. Without hope, they were just victims awaiting the slaughter. And that hope had been destroyed. He felt like joining Celia in shaking some sense back into Anne's head. Then he realized how selfish this attitude was. Anne couldn't help herself. He had to help her. He moved to pull Celia away. Anne was not resisting, and had gone quite limp.

With a metallic clatter, the key flew from Anne's blouse to the cage floor. Ed and Celia both stared at it, and Celia let Anne go. The keeper collapsed to the ground, obviously too stunned to move.

"It's real," Ed said, amazed. He'd been sure that Anne had imagined it, too.

"Yes." Celia pounced on it, and then screamed. The key had wound up close to the bars, and the tiger was staring at her from the other side, eyes bright, mouth wide, fangs dripping.

It's real, the tiger agreed. *As real as I am. And now that I know you have it, I'll be waiting until you use it.* The huge tongue moved. *I can be very patient.* Then it turned and moved away a few feet, where it sat, watching the cave.

Celia whimpered, clutching the key to herself like a charm to ward off evil. Ed felt like punching her.

"You idiot," he snarled. "Now they know we have the key, we'll never be able to use it. And it's all your stupid fault for being impatient! You've doomed us all, you moron." In disgust, he turned his back on her. He heard her sobbing, but he ignored her and moved as far away as he could get. His heart was as cold as ice, tight in his chest. Perhaps the key had been only a slight hope, but it had been a hope. Now, there was nothing. The animals hadn't even bothered to take it back; they had left it as a symbol of futility.

One of the men moved to where Celia was sobbing. "You jerk!" he screamed. "You've ruined it for us all!" He lashed out with his fist, knocking the girl to the ground.

Ed watched the man. For a horrifying moment he found himself wishing *he* was kicking Celia. After all, *she deserved it.* The lust to inflict pain overwhelmed him like a raw primitive instinct. Then, suddenly, he came to his senses. He grabbed the howling man by the wrist. The two men stood nose to nose. Ed looked into the other man's eyes. They were alive with hate and anger.

"Stop it!" Ed yelled.

The man twisted and struggled. Ed tightened his fist around the man's wrist. "I said stop it!" Celia had crawled across the cage and was cowering in the corner, whimpering. "It's wrong. We're not supposed to act like this."

The man looked at him with a blank stare. "Like what?"

"Like . . . animals."

CHAPTER 11

DEVRA WAS SCARED as she walked toward the center of the game farm. It was hard to believe that it was only a few short hours since she had walked in here, happily contemplating nothing but fun with her friends. Since then, the whole world seemed to have changed. Instead of watching her or harassing her for handouts of food, the deer were staring coldly. Maybe she was imagining their iciness, but they were certainly no longer friendly. It was hard to know what to read into those cold, staring eyes.

Heather whimpered, and Devra almost lost her nerve. Standing in their way was one of the brown bears. It had looked large enough in its cage, but now that it was in the open, it looked mountainlike. A huge mass of fur, paws, and muscle. And, when it opened its mouth, teeth.

What have you brought us here? Its voice was as massive and hard as the bear's body. Devra cringed.

Huntress didn't back down, though; she was a terrier, and terriers never seemed to be daunted by the size of a possible opponent. *These are my pets,* Huntress said. *I'm taking them to Penelope for approval.*

Devra still hated to be called a *pet,* but decided that it was definitely the wrong time to dispute the matter. The bear stared at the two girls, who clung to one another for comfort. Finally, it twitched its nose.

Well, I can always play with them later, it decided. Devra understood that "play with" meant "kill." She shivered. Huntress gave a mental sniff of disdain, and led the way past the bear. It deliberately didn't move, and they had to squeeze past it. Aside from the strong smell of bear, there was the stench of blood about the animal's fur. And it wasn't his own blood. It took all of Devra's nerve to force herself past the mountain of muscle. Once past it, they hurried on.

In the center of the game farm was the cluster of main cages that had once housed the tigers and bears. Now, however, they were filled with people, and the animals were outside. Heather gasped as they moved toward this.

"What have they done?" she whispered to Devra.

"Turned the world upside down," Devra replied. "And they're obviously enjoying this."

Humans, came a cold, hard voice in her mind. It made her want to scream and run, but she steeled her nerves and stared back at the tiger that was regarding her. The animal's tail was lashing, as if it were ready to charge.

They're with me, Huntress said, clearly not bothered by the icy hardness of the tiger.

So? The tiger padded forward to investigate.

So you had better not touch them, Huntress snapped angrily, *or I'll be very annoyed.*

Devra cringed. Surely the tiger wouldn't be bothered by that? They had been crazy to agree to come here. She and Heather would be killed; there was no way a small terrier could protect them from a beast like this.

Abruptly, the tiger laughed. It was an amused laugh, but still with that steel edge to it. *Very well,* it agreed. *I'd better not mess with you, obviously.* Devra could hear it chuckling to itself as it settled down again. But it kept its eyes firmly on them, following their every move.

"Heather! Devra!"

Devra looked at the cage they were passing. Inside, looking drawn and battered, was Ed, clutching the bars and staring in astonishment at them. "What are you doing here? I had hoped you'd escaped."

"It's the same all over," Devra replied. "The animals have taken over. They've got everybody captive. We've come to talk to Penelope, who seems to be in charge."

I am in charge, said a cold voice. A small monkey hopped onto the rim of a waste basket close by them. *What are you doing here?* She glared at Huntress. *Didn't I order all humans to be held captive until we needed them for food?*

Yes, Huntress agreed. *But these are my pets. I want to be allowed to keep them.*

Unthinkable! Penelope snapped. *Humans aren't pets.*

They're vicious, savage creatures, who enjoy inflicting pain on all animals. They must be replaced and destroyed, for all of our sakes.

Devra glared at the small monkey. "No we are not!" she said firmly. "I love animals. Ask Spice—er, Huntress. She'll tell you that I've always been good to her!"

It's true, Huntress backed her up. *She saved my life when I was abandoned by other humans, and she nursed me back to health. She feeds me and plays with me. She takes me for interesting walks. And she knows just how to scratch my tummy to make my leg thump.*

The monkey looked at the terrier coldly. *Obviously, you prefer the company of humans to that of your fellow animals, you traitor!* she snarled. *Do you want to end up like them? To share their fate? All humans are evil, and must be eradicated.*

"Says you," challenged Devra.

Yes, agreed Penelope. *And I know what I'm talking about. I have seen what you humans do to animals in the name of progress and science. You experiment with us, and dissect us. You give us drugs, and pain, and death. And you raise us simply to slaughter us, so you can eat our flesh. Well, the time has come for the payback—we shall do to you what you have done so long to us.*

"Not everyone is like that!" Devra yelled. "Yes, you've had some horrible things done to you. I can't deny that. But that's not true of everybody! Just a few people did that. You can't blame everyone for what those few did."

I can and I will, Penelope replied. *We shall never be safe while any humans live.*

"No," Heather broke in. "Devra's telling you the truth." She pointed at a deer with a white blaze on her forehead. "You—I remember you. Do you remember me? Haven't I always fed you when I come here? Been good to you?"

She has a point, the deer agreed. *I remember she was nice to me.*

The monkey spat on the ground. *One small kindness. And, tell me, who was it locked you in here against your will? Your parents? Other animals? Or humans?*

"Humans did it," Devra agreed. "But we treated them well. We loved them. And I love my dog. She loves me." She tried again. "You've had a horrible life, obviously. But ask around. Most of these animals haven't."

So you say, Penelope answered. *But they have been imprisoned, forced to work, and fed at your whim. They have never been free. And some of them were beaten and confined. Some have been killed. This is not a good life; it is mere existence. It is not enough to save your life.*

They were losing the argument, that much was clear. Penelope was too focused on the pains she'd suffered and witnessed to be able to think this through. She didn't want to be fair to people; she simply wanted revenge on them. There had to be *some* way to get through this. . . .

Devra pointed to the tiger. "What about you?" she challenged. "You want to kill and eat me. How does this make you any better than humans?"

It doesn't, the tiger answered lazily. *But I'm not in-*

terested in moral superiority. Only in physical superiority. It stretched, showing its lethal claws. *Do you think you could take me on and win?*

"Physically? No." Devra didn't want it thinking that way. "But you have no argument with humans, surely?"

Nor do I have any love for them, the tiger replied simply. *All I wish is to be free to hunt my food and go where I will. Humans have never allowed that.*

"But if they did, you would be happy?" Devra persisted. "You don't particularly want to see them wiped out, do you?"

It's a matter of utter indifference to me whether humans live or die, the tiger admitted.

"There you are," Devra said triumphantly, turning back to Penelope. "Even the tigers don't want to see the human race die. They just want to be free—which they are right now."

And for how long will they be free, if the humans are let loose? Penelope challenged. *They will get their guns and kill us, because they are afraid of us.*

"You have made them afraid," Heather pointed out.

Yes, agreed the monkey, with considerable satisfaction. *And we shall continue to make them afraid of us. You cannot win, because we are now as smart as you. And we have other advantages over you. We have sharper teeth and claws. We are stronger, swifter, more agile. Without your weapons, you humans are very puny indeed.*

"Maybe so," agreed Devra, as inspiration struck. "But it's not just our weapons that make us superior, you know.'' She held up her hand. ''We have opposable thumbs.''

Penelope held up her own. *So do I.* She sounded smug, but she'd walked into Devra's trap.

Devra looked at Huntress. ''And do you?'' she asked.

No, the terrier admitted. *But why would I need them?*

''Two words,'' said a fresh voice: ''can opener.''

Devra spun around. Two more people had come into the game farm, but they were not as helpless as the others. Both carried pistols, and the man looked like Rambo, with a rifle slung over his shoulder, and dressed in fatigues.

''Relax, gals,'' he said with a lazy grin. ''The U.S. Army is here now, and we'll take over.''

CHAPTER 12

GENERAL HALSEY LOOKED at his watch for the third time in as many minutes. There was a gnawing anxiety in his stomach he hadn't felt since Desert Storm. "Forty-four minutes," he grunted, more to himself than to his aide. "Come on, Alan . . ."

The circle of men stretched around him, now totally enclosing the town of Nolan. The buffer zone had been burned, and everybody stood by, waiting for time zero. There had been no reports yet of any animals trying to cross the zone. Either they were too scared or too intelligent to try, at least for now. It couldn't last, of course.

The missile had arrived, and was being held ready in a circling bomber. In forty-three minutes, Halsey would have to give the order to wipe out Nolan . . . if Alan didn't come through. Still, he had confidence: if anyone could save the town, it was Colonel Adair.

The problem was—*could* anyone save the town?

Adair moved forward, his senses on the alert. The two girls talking had occupied the attention of most of the animals, and he, Parker, and their doggy escort had managed to get this far without being challenged. Even the tiger hadn't been watching them come in.

Everything had changed now, of course. The animals focused in on him and Parker. The tiger moved to its feet, ready for a leap.

"Don't try it," Adair warned, moving his gun barrel very slightly. "I'm one of those nasty human beings who kills animals when it's called for. And you may have bigger claws than me, but I can shoot every one of them off your furry paws before you can even reach me."

The tiger stood watching it, saying nothing. It had to be smart enough to know he was telling the truth, but was it smart enough to care? Slowly, it seemed to uncoil, and some of the immediate tension evaporated.

Perhaps you can kill some of us with your weapons, human, the monkey said coldly, *but you cannot kill us all.*

"I don't have to kill any of you," Adair said cheerily. "I came here to talk, not to do the law of the jungle stuff. Kill or be killed. If you agree to talk, I won't shoot Tabby there."

You are very insolent, the tiger snapped. The voice

was powerful, but restrained. Adair had a suspicion he could get to like this character.

"Yeah, my mother raised me badly." Adair looked at the monkey. "I take it you're Penelope, the ringleader of this crazy circus. So, do you want to talk, or should I just start ventilating fur around here?"

We talk, agreed Penelope. She didn't sound enthusiastic though. *You are like all the humans I've ever known—a cold, merciless killer.*

"Trust me, I'm not like any human you've ever known," Adair promised. "And I kill only when I have to. I don't enjoy it—but I do it without hesitation." He didn't want any misunderstandings that he was weak. "Now, listen to the lovely lady. She's the diplomat. I'm just the soldier."

Parker gave him an odd look as she stepped forward. Significantly, she sheathed her pistol. Just as significantly, he didn't. "There is no need for this conflict," she said gently. "We can reach a compromise."

When humans say "compromise," they mean to cheat, Penelope answered. *We hold all of the advantages here. We have humans as hostages. You have nothing but a couple of guns.*

"You won't have humans for hostages very long," one of the young girls said. She was the dark-haired one that had been winning the argument earlier. Adair rather liked her. "Not if you keep letting the tigers kill them."

Smart girl, giving them information like that. "Hey, killing hostages is a no-no, fuzzy," Adair warned the monkey. "If any more die, I'm going to start retaliating. Understand me?"

"Adair, let me do the talking," Parker begged. He shrugged, and she turned back to the monkey. "The colonel is right, though; all killing stops now."

Or what?

"Or I let him loose. You've seen how efficient he can be." Parker took a deep breath. "There is room here for both of us to get what we want. You're trapped inside this town, and will never be allowed to leave."

You cannot stop us, Penelope replied.

"We can and we will," Parker answered. "There are soldiers surrounding the town. They have orders to kill any animal that tries to leave."

That stopped the monkey for a moment. Then she answered: *We have burrowers and others who can escape.*

"Given time," Parker agreed. "But you don't have time. You have"—she glanced at her watch—"less than forty minutes of life left to you."

What are you talking about? Penelope demanded. She sounded worried. Adair wasn't sure that this was the best route to take, but he had to trust Parker knew what she was doing.

"This town will be totally destroyed at the end of that period if we do not report that an agreement has been reached," she informed Penelope. "You know humans; you know we can do it."

The monkey stared at her and then at Adair. He grinned back. *You would kill your own, too?*

"They're dead if we leave them anyway, aren't they?" Parker pointed out. "You won't let them live. I'm sure they'd sooner die swiftly than wait to be killed off as tiger food."

Humans! Penelope spat out the word as a curse. *You always seek to destroy.*

"Hey, fuzz-face," Adair snapped. "All the killing around here has been done by you and your lackeys. But you'll soon discover that you're amateurs compared to the human race."

I suspect you are correct, agreed Penelope sadly.

"It doesn't have to be that way," Parker argued gently. "We can reach an understanding, and then I'll call off the attack. Nobody needs die."

What kind of understanding? asked the monkey bitterly. *We return to captivity? You experiment further with us?*

"No," Parker answered. "Look, I think you've all got human-level intelligence now. You have a right to a voice, a right to be heard. You should not be made captives again. That time is over. But you have to let these people go free and you have to agree not to fight or kill again."

Why should we believe you? Penelope asked.

"Actually, because you have no choice," the agent replied. "It's either accept what I tell you, or die."

"Besides which," Adair couldn't resist adding, "you really don't have any better plan, do you? I mean, what did you expect to do once you'd wiped out this town?

Just move on and do it again and again?" He laughed. "You would never have gotten away with it. There's not enough of you, for one thing."

There will be more soon, Penelope promised.

"Like heck there will." Adair shrugged. "At some point you will have used up all of the BZT. And once you're out of the magic elixir, that means no reinforcements, since only we humans can make it."

I know how to do it, Penelope argued.

"Yeah, and I know how to fly," he snapped. "But I can't flap my arms and do it. And you can't make BZT without help. And without the stuff, you're doomed. For all you know, the effects may wear off in a week. And there's no way your kids will be born smart without it. Face it, you're the entire Animal Liberation Army right now, and there's never going to be any more. We know what caused you, and it will never happen again."

"And there's another way that there's no future," Parker added. She couldn't resist grinning at Adair. "Two words: can opener."

What do you mean? Penelope sounded very disturbed now.

"What are you going to feed yourselves on with no humans around?" the agent asked. She gestured to the dark-haired girl. "As she was saying, you need opposable thumbs to open cans of cat and dog food. And, though you have the thumbs, you don't have the strength to turn the can openers. So, no food."

"Right," Adair agreed. "Oh, the deer can do fine

grazing. But I don't think Tabby the tiger there is going to live on grass. Once the people are gone, what's he going to eat? You?''

"And the dogs and cats," the dark-haired girl added. "They normally eat smaller animals. Are you going to get volunteers to die to keep your troops alive?'' Adair was liking the kid more all the time.

The monkey was out of its depth, and had to be realizing it about now. She looked nervously around, obviously thinking about what had been said.

"Come on," Parker said gently. "There's no way you can win if you insist on fighting. You'll all die in thirty minutes. If you try running, you'll be killed. The only thing left to you is to give up your hatred for now and come to terms. We can be reasonable.''

Reasonable? Penelope screamed. *I've seen what humans do! They lie, they cheat, and they kill! We can't trust any of you!*

I can, said a terrier, stepping forward. *I trust my girl. If she promises to be good to me, I know she will be. I love her.*

"Thank you, Huntress," the dark-haired girl said, bending to scratch the terrier's head. "I knew you'd be smart.''

"What about the rest of you?'' Parker called, looking around. The animals were all looking concerned and confused. "Penelope seems to prefer hatred to sense. But are the rest of you as determined to die? Or are you willing to talk?''

I don't want to die, one of the deer called out. *Now that I can think, I want to live on.*

As do I, the tiger agreed. *I see no shame in talking with humans. As long as it is as an equal.*

"You seem like an equal to me, pal," Adair said, grinning. "Trust me, I wouldn't sit at a table with you and try and lie."

There was further discussion, cut short by Penelope. *No!* she howled. *These are* humans! *They cannot be trusted! We have to stay together and fight!*

Parker shook her head. "You've all developed intelligence," she called loudly. "You have brains: use them! Don't listen only to her hatred of humans! Think for yourselves, now that you can! Make your own minds up!"

The dogs were the first to move away. *We can trust people,* a malamute decided. *We will talk.*

As will I. The tiger moved closer to where Adair stood. He felt momentary alarm, but then settled down, knowing that the animal had no need to lie. You had to have a respect for a creature like this.

What can you promise us? one of the bears asked. *What will you give us?*

"I don't know," Parker said, honestly. "These things will have to be talked over. But I can promise you that we all won't die if we can agree to talk. And if you set the people free."

No! Penelope yelled. *We cannot give in to the humans! They will trick us and lie to us and kill us!*

They will kill us anyway if we do not agree, the tiger

said. *There is no advantage in fighting such a war. We shall talk, even if you do not wish it.*

Never! Penelope screamed. Then she threw herself at Parker, ready to rip off her face.

Adair and the tiger moved at the same second. Adair's first shot caught the monkey in mid-leap. He was forced to hold his fire, though, as the tiger caught the screaming primate in its mouth and bit down.

The screaming stopped. The tiger opened its mouth, dropping the crushed body to the ground.

Now, he said, *we can talk. The war is over.*

"Thank God," Adair said, fervently. He unslung his radio, and turned it on. "Adair to Halsey, code umber."

"Halsey here," came the immediate reply. The general's voice was both tense and eager. "What's the word?"

"Two words: *stand down.*" Adair grinned.

"Affirmative." The relief was extremely clear in Halsey's voice. "You have the situation under control?"

"Well, it's not that simple," Adair confessed. "We have some . . . negotiating to do. And you may have problems with our fellows on this. But I think we'll be able to do just fine. You can start coming in, but without naked weapons. Adair out." He turned to the tiger. "I'm not sure how they're going to like my solution, but they'll abide by it. I promise."

The tiger grinned mentally. *And I will make sure of it. For now, though* . . . he turned to the remaining monkeys, *release the humans. It is over.*

Adair felt a huge sense of relief. It was going to be very, very strange working with intelligent animals. But life would be very, very interesting. He moved forward to the young girl. "Nice work," he told her. "You're a smart kid."

"I'm *not* a kid," she snapped. Then she managed a wan grin. "Were you bluffing about that bomb? Would you really have killed us all?"

"Yes," he answered honestly. He gestured at the cages, which the animals were starting to open. "Would you have wanted this to spread?"

"No," she agreed. "I wouldn't. It would have been the right thing to do." Then she grinned again. "And I'd have hated you for it!"

"Heather! Devra!" A teenaged boy hurried over from one of the cages, and hugged the two girls. "Are you both okay?"

"We are now." Devra watched as the people filed silently out of the cages. "They don't look very happy to be rescued, Ed."

"Honestly," Ed admitted, "most of them aren't very proud of themselves. I think we need a doctor or two in here, sir," he added to Adair. "A couple of people were injured. One girl was beaten up. Another seems to have gone mad."

"I'm sure there will be medics coming in," Adair promised. He turned to Parker. "So, do you know any good restaurants around here?"

Parker looked at the animals. "Maybe we can find a good vegetarian place?" she suggested.

Adair nodded. "Maybe we can." Everything had changed indeed. And it wasn't over yet.

What would happen next?

EPILOGUE

Everything had changed, now. No longer could a human being consider himself or herself to be the pinnacle of creation. Animals who can think like people are a new species. Can the human race get along with them? If so, what will they gain? And what will they have to give up? And if they can't get along—will there be another war? Mankind against the rest of the animal kingdom? Who would win such a war?

When things change so radically, the consequences are difficult to see . . . except that the future will become even more interesting than usual.

TOR BOOKS

Check out these titles from Award-Winning Young Adult Author
NEAL SHUSTERMAN

Enter a world where reality takes a U-turn...

MindQuakes: Stories to Shatter Your Brain

"A promising kickoff to the series. Shusterman's mastery of suspense and satirical wit make the ludicrous fathomable and entice readers into suspending their disbelief. He repeatedly interjects plausible and even poignant moments into otherwise bizzare scenarios...[T]his all-too-brief anthology will snare even the most reluctant readers."—*Publishers Weekly*

MindStorms: Stories to Blow Your Mind

MindTwisters: Stories that Play with Your Head

And don't miss these exciting stories from Neal Shusterman:

Scorpion Shards

"A spellbinder."—*Publishers Weekly*

"Readers [will] wish for a sequel to tell more about these interesting and unusual characters."—*School Library Journal*

The Eyes of Kid Midas

"Hypnotically readable!"—*School Library Journal*

Dissidents

"An involving read."—*Booklist*

Call toll-free 1-800-288-2131 to use your major credit card or clip and mail this form below to order by mail

- -

Send to: Publishers Book and Audio Mailing Service
PO Box 120159, Staten Island, NY 10312-0004

☐ 55197-4	**MindQuakes**	$3.99/$4.99 CAN	☐ 52465-9 **Scorpion Shards**	$4.99/$5.99 CAN
☐ 55198-2	**MindStorms**	$3.99/$5.50 CAN	☐ 53460-3 **The Eyes of Kid Midas**	$4.99/$5.99 CAN
☐ 55199-0	**MindTwisters**	$3.99/$4.99 CAN	☐ 53461-1 **Dissidents**	$3.99/$4.99 CAN

Please send me the following books checked above. I am enclosing $_____. (Please add $1.50 for the first book, and 50¢ for each additional book to cover postage and handling. Send check or money order only—no CODs).

Name _____

Address _____ City _____ State _____ Zip_____